In the Animal Kingdom

In The Animal Kingdom

by Warren Fine

Alfred A. Knopf New York 1971

THIS IS A BORZOI BOOK
PUBLISHED BY ALFRED A. KNOPF, INC.

Copyright © 1971 by Warren Fine

All rights reserved under International and Pan-American
Copyright Conventions. Published in the United States by
Alfred A. Knopf, Inc., New York, and simultaneously in
Canada by Random House of Canada Limited, Toronto.
Distributed by Random House, Inc., New York.

ISBN: 0–394–46969–0

Library of Congress Catalog Card Number: 77–142954

Manufactured in the United States of America

An early version of part of this story appeared in
The Mill Creek Valley Intelligencer *under the title "Gerhard 1779."*

FIRST EDITION

For John Hawkes

One

In America, I throw my single voice about like a ventriloquist; like an evangelist—ox, eagle, ass, or winged man—I play my various tongues, both intimate and distant voices cast from my mouth, as if fishlines spread to flickering sheets, become so much like fish themselves, like blades and flames, to catch my experience in the animal kingdom, to come into my story, feeling as if with my tongue, to know again, and know mostly now, the process of my adventure in the flesh, as all tongues, like castaways returning through my mouth, reenter and descend into my present body.

I remembered the past and projected even the future death of myself, as I took my journey among companions— four men, and one woman as singular as my voice—from the Wabash to dry plainsland, as fire and earth came from the dark ocean, remembering here how I then seemed to hear the voices, seemed to remember, and to project myself, how I dreamed and envisioned my new world, now feeling I can re-create a former order in the mind, of experience, as if I could only experience it now, as if the old order never exists until it issues, like a new creature, from my mouth.

I remember, among changes of my tongue, those other tongues or voices emerging as if I died into them, out of my imagined death in time, rehearsing them now as I remember I heard them, in the order of memory, as I hear or speak them to myself, as if in long quotations, long sounds like pleadings, as if men become their breaths on the air or become my diaphragm, lungs, teeth, tongue, lips, my mouth, this worded breath flowing out like water too long forgotten about, my companions lodged in my voice as if in my body they entered a friend's house, and I speak their speech as if all language were my own.

What I remember then, happens now, when I remember the ocean, gray as if dying, which left me high and dry on the American shore; crossing mountains, little homesteads in the clearings; furniture and guns, wood and metal work-

ing; and the ocean a February land had become, when Mississippi and Wabash swelled over their tributaries, almost merging under the rain, as sky and earth became almost one muddy, watery substance, as the Ohio rose, never quite arriving from the south; and myself in the overland journey of that winter, from Kaskaskia to Vincennes, west to east as if under the rivers, expecting any morning, waking, to be transformed—the shiny scales, the pulse of new gills, fins like black limber bones forked from merged buttocks and erect on my spine—traveling through the flooding ground; now I remember before the spring journey: under the moon, a river, a grove: remember.

There was something of ritual in the pattern four young men and I, one boy, made under the small moon, in the high grove's clearing, above the dwindling river. One man, just a large shape, looming out of the horses and trees, held the horse he could have tied and said to light the brush piles; so the other two men, holding the flares far from dimmed heads, leaned, and bent their fires to brush they'd gathered, establishing a line about one hundred feet long, perfectly bisected by another drawn from the horseholder to the first line. An almost ideal intersection existed where Captain Cantrell and I, German Boy or Dutch, stood together stiffly, back to back, elbows crooked and pistol barrels poised upright near thrust-out chins. I imagined that the second line darted through the little hole at our napes, or slid between the conjunction of our spines and buttocks. I could imagine Cantrell as he was: small and slight, long-muscled; reminiscent, in daylight if not in this dark, of a silver fox.

There was the clearing and ritual formations—the

dark, still figures against horses and trees, and Cantrell with me—these patterns I was aware we made before I was aware of nothing but small steps the horse-sub-duer numbered loudly in bellowing shouts, like an elephant trumpeting, and of the little brush of fire I was shoving into; so I was slow to turn when the signal came, and Cantrell must have known I was slowed. One instant too long that fire behind me, tiny green flames curled into themselves like closed buds the bushes thrust into the world, remained in my eyes when I changed, whirling, cocking the handgun, while I couldn't see Cantrell under the thin moon, could see nothing but the flickering signs of fire behind me, in the eyes still, and then the fire like mine behind Cantrell, as if I stood between two mirrors reflecting flames; until brightly, in changing starless night, his original blond of hair and beard came redder and more blue than I'd ever known my own red hair or my own blue eyes to be.

I aimed where I thought his heart was, and I fired through dim alternating colors of bushlit night. I could see his small dark outline more clearly then. Cantrell was rushing on me, a quickening fury of bones and skin and muscles, flamelike—in a flurry as of a fighting cock sudden in feathers—and only then did I know, staring helplessly in the face of his rush, he had fired his only shot, contemptuously, into the ground, into April's wet earth, taking my own lightly in his left shoulder.

All this I knew I'd seen then. There was the grove, of ash and bur oak, there was the clearing of broken or transfigured ritual, and Cantrell's pistol barrel, in his right hand, lashing, and Cantrell's eyes flared high above his beard, before I sank, lifting my discharged pistol (so heavy now as I fell) as if I owned that extra, primed, impossible ball, to repudiate my enemy. I wondered at this sinking, losing my time, like a tent pole pounded slowly down unwinding entrails of the thawing, April underworld. Then, without surprise, I believed I heard an ultimate vengeance executed on my head, as if in the voice we spoke with once, in the watery journey.

We said, "*February fifth,* 1779, the bateau, we call her the *Willing,* is finished and loaded, together with ammunition and two four-pounders and four swivels we dispatch her with forty-six men, we raise another company to make our number now 170 men and about three o'clock after receiving a lecture and absolution from a popish preacher we cross the Kaskaskia River with our baggage leaving two men in the fort, we advance about a league from the town, the officers and some few others on horseback have an easy time yet the baggage is long in transporting, the weather is not cold for this season however drizzly, one company is sent on horseback to acquire more game from the prairie and scattered woods, some of us cut cane poles casting lines in the river passing many jokes, two men capture fish by hand in the shallow pools, much gaiety to see them running after the small fish and tadpoles, Colonel Clark laughing so hard at us, the fishermen at the banks forgetting their lines and cares, all in good spirits this day, we are full of anticipation, the colonel so cheerful with us."

I said to myself, "I am not dead yet." I saw myself in the dream and said, "That is not me. It is nothing like me." The boy, who was like me, the boy I saw, stepped up, three inches, on a three-legged stool, and bent to fart at the sun. Still bending, he blew smoke gently to the earth. The sun filled up three quarters of the sky and rolled about the boy's horizon, randomly winking, white to blue, returning to white. When the white sun shone, it sucked pollen from the flowers it had raised; and, turning blue, it lingered, in odors of night. When the sun shone white, while he shook as if cold, he was clothed entirely in wintry furs—beaver fur, mink, and buffalo. When, suddenly, the sun cooled, coolness starting from its long, blue mouth, like a hare startled from cover, as late spring freeze rained down on his flesh, the red-haired boy went naked, sweating. Darkened by my dream, he fanned himself with white leaves; roses smothered his smelly feet. He always wore, beginning then, the old black hat with two long peaks, like ass or rabbit ears, while an unseen audience, a sophisticated animal crowd, both laughed and wept. Smiling, now at ease, he shot a musketball into the crowd, which boomeranged to pink him in the ass. He swallowed a talking, vegetable laxative and, rising swiftly sunward on the pile, destroyed a village with his ancient shit. The whole scene joined somehow, for the dreamer, for me, with stories that a half-breed told me recently, his tribal stories interspersed with others; and I recognized the village, a Siberian town I'd stayed three months in once with my journeyman father. Meanwhile, in the dream, the boy lay a large and decorative egg, split it carefully, washed the sun's hair with its yoke, and whirled the egg white into trout like rainbows. To a rhythm of laughter and tears from the invisible but attentive throng, he became a young woman or girl, carefully framed, and, lifting a loin cloth, revealed five tiny cunts. He told a dirty joke and several lies, while a red fox jumped him cunt by cunt; the fox brush caused, then put a stop to, each flow of blood. He changed, in return, and struck the other boy he thought lay hidden beneath the water, shattered his own reflection with a consequent fall, and died, only to be washed ashore, alive, on the pool's small evening or morning tide. When the sun came white, he dressed and went to bed. When the sun went blue, he waited to wake in the night, in skins as hairless as the flesh he came in. At last, the boy I was in the dream agreed with something the dreamer had said, "Oh no, I am not dead yet!"

My name was Gerhard, in buckskins still and brown, Gerhard Blau or German Boy or Dutch. Patterning the ground, unconscious from the captain's blows, I lay, George Clark's youngest trooper, on April's runny ground, while the moon in its starless night turned a new gold sliver of leaf among the clouds, above Fort Sackville, above Vincennes, Illinois Country, 1779. Nearby me, three young men waited on my waking. Sergeant Orcus Berrigan still held the horses, only four now, though he could have tied them, while Privates Packer Smith and Oscar Thomson knelt at the side of Gerhard Blau, only heir, eighteen, of an Essen carpenter and gunsmith, and of an English mother.

Almost invisible in darkness above the river, the three men watched me while my spirit was indifferent to them, to their existence. They saw my body now by moonlight only, in fireless night, while the bush fires scarcely smoldered. Fragmentarily, the dream in me lingered when I woke, as if it would continue in the waking mind. Silently, avoiding the approach of their eyes, I squatted before the men and shook my head gently, weaving slightly, touched two fingers to the drying blood on my face and hair, and listened a moment to the horses snuffling.

Knowledge of English, of my mother's language, I'd left in the dream I was leaving; yet I understood that Berrigan asked me something, one insistent, repeated question. Smith and Thomson, lost among the heads of the vague snorting animals, spoke a totally inhuman language, babbling; but I heard them speak the name of the captain.

Berrigan bent toward me from the horses, from Smith and Thomson; his face—heavily fleshed, especially his great nose upon the large bones—obscured by his thick beard, like an elephant hidden in the undergrowth, these features of Berrigan emerged from the horses, so slowly, out of a background of bare, dark, tangled branches, his countenance descending, said for the boy to lie back down again. So I was aware of Berrigan and knew him, and also knew they'd moved me from the place I'd fallen, toward the trees, near the horses standing before the trees; for I could hear the horses tearing the long grass with their teeth, dipping their heads and lifting them among the tree trunks.

In my passion, I couldn't speak English before the young men, especially before Smith and Thomson, whose smooth dark heads were revealed often by the long-necked dipping of the horses' heads; so I enunciated carefully, "Ein. Jahr. Oder. Mehr." I meant only that it had been a year or more since I'd come to America; I didn't know why I thought that would be an answer. I heard more words, some of which I repeated quietly to myself, trying to understand them, "Mount up now . . . Dutch . . . make our number . . . bullion . . . water." Berrigan, whose words they were I'd repeated, spoke loudly toward me, bending from the other young men, asking if I understood, then something about pulling out, across a big river near Kaskaskia, something about gold again. I nodded my head eagerly, brightening though I couldn't have understood yet about the bullion they'd captured from the British and hidden from Clark, nor could've precisely known what was happening to me now. I guessed, mostly from what Berrigan said, arguing with the others, that they meant to cross the Mississippi near Kaskaskia, after doing something about gold, crossing into Spanish territory to descend the river.

I knew I wanted to leave Vincennes now, to depart from the place where I was, no matter what. A notion of Cantrell flared inside me, like the bush fires; it could wait, I felt, a century or two. I was becoming slowly more than just the pain in my head or the humiliation in my breast, more than my dream, yet for the moment my eyes subsided, as if into trance, into a childish madness, and I said, "Der Fluss . . . uber den Fluss." Then I thought that if I was afraid of Cantrell it didn't matter, and I wondered if Berrigan knew I meant to kill Cantrell one day, and I thought it could wait.

Smith or Thomson, nearing Berrigan, said that he didn't want something, and Berrigan asked Smith or Thomson, sharply, what it was he didn't want. The argument was brief. Berrigan said that maybe he liked the German boy. Then Smith and Thomson accepted the reins of the horses they'd been riding, the borrowed horses, and they waited on horseback.

I stood up. The top of the tree that Berrigan was under seemed to swing around the horses' heads. For the first time that night I noticed the sky roughened and dark; and the stars now appearing, to set deeply into the clouds, like tiny jewels in the nap of a rug.

Smith or Thomson asked what about Cantrell, whose plan it was. Berrigan asked what Cantrell had done for them, waiting so long. He walked the remaining two horses toward me, looming, while Smith and Thomson thought it all over and one or both of them decided Cantrell had done nothing for them. Berrigan asked me if I could ride now.

"Doch!" I cried, and mounted to prove it.

Berrigan, whose head was almost level with mine, studied us all from the ground, nodded, and rose. His bones were so big they seemed about to emerge from his flesh, revealing another man inside him. He said to ride, settling his spine in the saddle, soon riding ten yards ahead.

I startled my companions with a whoop, and shouted, "Zum Fluss, also!" I heard Berrigan laugh up ahead, urging his young sorrel stallion into a canter, heard Smith and Thomson plunging after me. We swung the horses south, circling to avoid the fort.

This April passage wasn't ever so wet as the February crossing was, but the new world thawed muddy, clouds hung up, and horses slogged through swamp and drizzle, till the third night when stars occasionally poked out and earth refroze beneath the hoofs. On the fifth night, snow, down separated areas of sky, fell in long streaks, like isolated clusters of a woman's hair. Then for two days it was clear, it was cold, and the prairie seemed crisp and fragile, the stiffened grass hoary up to the knees of our horses. The spell broke on the seventh day, and each succeeding morning ascended warmer than the previous morning. We kept to the dry high ground where we could, but streams still flooded, and Berrigan scouted ahead our fords.

Cantrell meshed against my mind. I knew relief, mixed with regret, at leaving behind an enemy at the fort. On the eighth day I realized I'd deserted, and put it behind me. I imagined the other three progressed through various images of Cantrell's vengeance, felt the captain shift, as I felt, in a semicircle through the north, with the wind, to blow from the west in breaths of spring. The first night I had slept against my horse's neck, while my recent dream seemed represented by a variation:

A small young girl, approximately thirteen, climbed a budding tree and swayed in its windy top. Her white shift whipped and snarled about her body, while a swift, short-winged hawk circled and dived repeatedly above the tree, emitting, like a bat, short, periodic shrieks. The blond girl leaned an ear against the whir of dives, and studied the high, monotonous circles that wings, gone vague, gone vaguer, described above the branches. The sky, containing that bird above the treetop and the girl, arched over the earth like a woman rising from a man.

At first I didn't recognize myself in the dream, and never made any precise identification. I imagined I might be a tree with a girl in me. She swayed in my branches, she stirred, and small twigs, fragmenting, and small buds, bursting, spun down their fall from my sides and arms. Or I was earth beneath the sky's departing body, and the sky as yet one with the earth, that sky a circling bird was winding up. Or I was earth-sky and the bird my soul, indwelling like the girl in her new leaves. Or I was, externally, that invisible, possibly dark sun which illuminated the scene. Or I, Gerhard, was simply the as yet whole scene, with what was in it. Or just some simple combination of simple things, like a missing sun and the present dream.

At least in the dream I felt the matter simply put. I felt night overcome me, and saw the star-rise sparkling up into the sky's body. The moon hid now, as the sun had before the moon. Then there was something quite ridiculous in the thing, and my three companions must have heard me laugh, urging horses into visions of their own.

Twice that first night, in a fine dizziness, a silky web, I had fallen from my bay and wakened; then Berrigan bound my ankles and hands with sinews, under the mare's brown belly and around her neck, and returned to his own progress, I imagined, toward a further vision of dark, probably Spanish women, sunlit by bars of gold.

On the first morning, the others killed a hare, and we sat in shadows, resting. I imagined Smith and Thomson whispered to each other as they wondered what Cantrell and I had fought for. They hadn't bothered to find out; they shrugged their shoulders. The two young men would be dead. They wouldn't find out; in this April earth, they wouldn't discover.

We said, "*February eighth, 1779,* we march early through the waters several inches deep, very difficult and fatiguing, we make a good march of about nine hours, we pitch our camp out of the mud and water at last on an eggshell hill, every company to guard its own square, we are so exhausted from traversing large and level plains where from the flatness of the country and the high grass water rests a considerable time before it drains off, we are suffered by the colonel to shoot game, he says on all occasions we may, tonight one company plays the host to all the others, this company which will receive us at night riding horses far supplying us with game while we who guard the supplies become sleepy watching the fish tangled in their weeds or grasses, the cane poles waver over the flooded land, the evening comes before very long, we feast on the fresh game like Indian war dancers, one hand filled with food while another waves in the damp air, we feel like kings and princes, we believe in ourselves, we hope we will have such feasting every night of the journey, having once tasted such meat, beast, fowl, and fish, thanking God for Colonel Clark's liberality, the colonel and his officers shouting in mud and water, running among the nervous horses, beating up the pretended game cocks, harrying imaginary foxes, putting on the pretense of woodsmen, and we eat heartily of hare and grouse and fish and we share a pointed deer, the curious turning of his branched head as the stars come up, all in such good spirits as the diversions of this night produce a forgetfulness in us of this day we have endured, the long march, but tonight we are men among men, the colonel like an angel to us also his officers ministering, this night is the best many of us have ever known.

"*February twelfth,* 1779, march across Cot Plains, we see and kill a few buffaloes from a small herd drifted eastward, our gun shots crackling in the air like the lightning while the buffalo thunder matches the brooding thunder of the purple skies, they plow the prairie up in dying slides, for a time we feel lost among the brutes, they are like hoofed whales that live upon the land, monstrous sharp-horned creatures, really terrible to us, we must kill them, we ride, those of us who kill, through the fetlock-deep water, the buffaloes seem to float a moment in death then slide like plows into the watery earth, their blood welling up very dark-colored like the mud, we camp upon the site, on a hillock and it is late in the evening before the baggage joins us, we eat the strong meat, one of the calves, the flesh of the hump especially tender and good, while the colonel like a merciful schoolmaster speaks to us about the Indians and the buffalo and freedom, then he appears very tired walking from the camp alone as we dress the hides, we are sorry for him and swear among ourselves to forever be faithful."

Now the other young men had busy hands: Berrigan pawed the stallion's ears, talking, preparing him, as if molding the head; Smith pinched the earth with forefingers and thumbs, released the grasped earth upon itself, pinched, released again; while Thomson whittled a twig from the maple, gray revealing green revealing white interior wood. Only *my* hands were still. I watched Smith and Thomson squatting in the tree's shadow. I studied the sky.

The sun, declining slowly, was like an eye that watched us, and she, the brown mare, stood in the tall grass with me, while I could feel her jaws working in my palms. Otherwise she was still as I faced her, as my hands were still. Some high geese passed northward before me, between me and the sun.

The mare stood where I'd tied her to the small shrub. I held her head low, looked back into her eyes, which were inpenetrable and brown. In this moment, I felt myself alone with her, set off from Berrigan, who, like the bear in his name, led his young horse forward, and felt also apart from the shrunken men under the tree. I would have liked to know what lay behind the eyes she raised to me. She seemed so unconcerned, her patience too extreme: only the tremors through her jaws assured me she cared.

Her heat had been more evident on the trail, as

she'd stroked against the moving flanks of the other horses. It was Berrigan who insisted we stop, so near the Mississippi, on the tenth day.

Smith and Thomson, spaniel-eyed, squatted and smirked near the maple, in shadow; Berrigan's stallion, in his initiation, had already failed the mare once, though she'd been so helpful, adjusting to his thrust. Berrigan had to pull him off her flank. The penises of horses, so long and wet and hot, had always shocked me, but the mare seemed almost indifferent to his lust, despite her movements, indifferent to her own need.

Now she waited, opaque eyes low and staring, as if intentionally unrevealed; now she waited for another approach of the stallion. And I wondered in what way she was aware of him that she wasn't aware of me. All my life I'd known horses, yet the mare remained like an animal emerging from my dreams, so near and alien.

Here was the mare standing as mares had before; here Berrigan and the stallion reapproaching as I watched them. Here was the stallion, mounted and tiresomely missing until the mare, shoved toward me, discovered herself to him. His purple flanks heaving, he penetrated, only to miss again on the next stroke. Through late afternoon air, his white seed steaming in long spurts departed toward whatever directions he accidentally thrust; while the mare shoved her head down sharply through my hands, and grazed quietly, as if what she'd received, in the inept but sufficient performance, had meant nothing beyond the act itself. She seemed now even calmer, more peaceful.

Berrigan tied the young horse, still nervy, to the maple, a solitary tree, where Smith and Thomson stood now, laughing in small barks. I remained where I was before the mare, studied her chewing, the green juice flowing slippery over her jaws, her lids which sealed already sealed eyes.

I noticed my palms were sweaty, and I discovered a tremor in myself, like lightning slow along the bones, fire twining, a shudder, as if the experience of horses continued, the shock meant always for me only. I remembered the invisible observing animals from my dream in the grove. Somehow, in that overland journey, I'd come into a life I hadn't expected, as though startled from dreams.

That night, even in darkness, the horses grew clearer —white, red, black, and muddy brown—more visible when I'd learned of the mare and the stallion. Four distinct horses approached a cabin set among tree stumps on the edge of a wood.

On the white and black horses, Smith and Thomson flanked me. They were also more apparent, as though through their horses. I knew them somehow false, my natural enemies, these dogged yellow-eyed riders, unnatural on horseback, dismounting now, like hounds on the spoor of gold bars, whose tongues licked their glistening mouths.

The Frenchman appeared in the doorway of his cabin, obscuring his wife who held a candle over his shoulder, over the blue glow of her hair. He was a small puffy man with pinched nostrils and a merry smile, pointed black mustaches which flickered like negatives of the bright candleflame.

It was the female voice that said, sharply, in English, to come in, and, when the trapper pivoted aside to admit his visitors, his departed body revealed her pressed against the door, her head inclined toward us, eyes down, as though she listened to music. She seemed, in the doorway, no older than I was. She wore a white cotton dress with blue trim at the wrists and neck; a black pattern zigzagged through the blue. She seemed so careless, the way she held the candle, the Indian girl, her flesh and eyes looked soft and brown, brown Indian flesh so soft upon broad features, brown eyes so soft surrounded by whiteness, I felt I could sink carelessly, myself, into either eyes or features. I passed by.

The men talked, in mixed French and English, about the gold and a route down the river. I watched her secretly as she lay, like a young doe, on a pile of rags in one dark corner. She appeared to be sleeping, while I desired her. The candle stood on the table where the three men talked, and I continued to lean against the wall behind Berrigan, to watch the girl who seemed to change before me. In repose, outside the light, she'd begun to look older, which I felt brought her closer.

The Frenchman brought out an accordion and, as he made a few preliminary noises, the woman rose and left the cabin, to reappear with a dark jug which we passed from mouth to mouth. I sat down to the table and drank long draughts, as even the Indian woman did. It was some kind of berry wine I'd never tasted. It pierced the flesh inside my mouth like small hot blades.

The Indian woman, who they called both Sawpoot-way and Marie, brought another brown jug from outdoors, and we began to dance drunkenly. The Frenchman smiled all the time he squeezed the instrument or let it out, as the rest of us took turns dancing. Then the Frenchman, Jacques LeGuey, laid down the pleated instrument and danced with his wife.

As I looked at the husband jealously, Berrigan laughed loudly and caught me in a bear hug. Smith and Thomson began to throw each other about, often falling, rolling over each other; they drank from additional jugs they'd brought inside from the spring. I was spun round, almost invisibly in Berrigan's grasp, wishing his concealing arms were the woman's. I believed she watched me; I believed she'd watched all along, pretending not to.

The men made me dance with her, while they stood and watched, and I believed she was happy dancing with me. Drunkenly, I threw her around the room, and she laughed and cried out to her husband, in the husband's language, pretending I'd hurt her; but I believed she'd waited for me, doe-like, in the flickering corner shadows. She showed no sign to me, becoming drunker it seemed, though she'd stopped drinking. I believed she'd forgotten to drink, dancing with me.

LeGuey drifted away then. He removed his breeches and curled up on the pile of rags to sleep. He raised his knees against his chest, and I saw his deep red bottom under his blouse, his genitals sagging purple behind him. Giggling, Smith and Thomson fell to hands and knees, sniffed, lifted their heads unnaturally, and held their noses for a long time. Neither Berrigan nor I laughed at their antics, as we watched the woman cover her husband with a deerskin.

The sleeping man and I remained, but the others disappeared and I couldn't remember them leaving. She'd gone without giving me a sign, and now the sun of the eleventh day was rising, fleecy like a lamb, powerful like the lamb's father. Standing in the doorway, I saw the sun become as red, on the horizon, as Jacques LeGuey's bottom.

I left the cabin, passed the sleeping horses standing in the stump-laden ground, and found the stream about a hundred yards into the wood. I improvised a tune to myself softly, as yet a wordless tune, and heard, as I was long without my sleep, another voice echoing my own, as if in accompaniment, though no one else was present to speak or sing. I stopped my song suddenly, and caught the companion voice continuing beyond mine for an instant. I'd quit walking. Of course I knew that it was my own voice tinnily doubled. I added words to my tune, senseless words, and heard them doubled with the tune. I stopped the song and heard the continuance. I was silent then, listening, after all but birdsong had stopped. The treetops above the sycamores, pillars of ivory, seemed to disintegrate into the rising sun, while I remained in night time by the water. Sleepily, I lowered myself onto the shelf of rock until my head entered the stream. I listened, while in this other medium, for a sound that could be fish talking, but heard only the stream's own rush, the hum of my ears, my blood pulsing. I slept on the limestone shelf, under the sycamore branches.

After my journey with Sir Robert to the Hebrides, those western islands, I had gone from England to the continent and Essen, to the house in which my mother died, taking that opportunity to see my first home before I returned to the sea again to meet Captain Wilson's ship and sail away.

As we moved away to sea, the Flanders coast, the land breaking away from the sea that bloomed in me, had seemed, in discriminating sunlight, a significant line of departure: the sea, green-blue, reflected the English ship, *Augusta,* the passenger faces among flowers—of men and women, of children uplifted along the rail, while a land breeze blew us toward the Channel.

In midvoyage, the sky, which on the first day of the sea journey lay open, like a pale rose in blue water, its clouds displayed like petals, became a complex, cloud-hedged maze of a garden, a difficult labyrinth.

I was Hiram Wilson's cabin boy, and I stayed much in the cabin where I did what work there was. Often I wrote in my journal about the recent trip to Scotland:

"It was now eleven o'clock in the darkest of nights, and I suddenly seemed, for only an instant, to see myself as if from afar—a pale, glowing figure, as though like a sea creature phosphorescent, alone on the deck of the tattered vehicle, raged about by the dark, my white figure alone thrust out in a kind of defiance at the ocean's storm. Of course the next instant my vision seemed silly, as I realized again the presence of the other men on board, and as I then saw them all busy, even Mr. Joseph, I considered it my sin that I alone was idle, in my solitary, selfish thoughts, while such a tumult was upon us among these islands, a terrible storm as if, in that southeast wind, Europe, with Asia and Africa behind, burst in disintegrating surges upon our heads, a sin that I alone should stand apart, as if I alone could withstand that heaven-sent landfall, and I asked Coll, with much earnestness and apology for stunned inactivity, what I could do to help preserve our lives. He, with a happy readiness, put into my hand a rope, which was fixed to the top of one of our masts, and told me to hold it till he bade me pull. If I had considered this matter in the undertaking of it, I might have seen that this could not be of the least service; but his object was to keep me out of the way of those who were busy working the vessel, and at the same time to divert my great fear, which he must have known from his own experience, by employing me, and making me think I was thereby of use, when

I was not. Thus did I, ignorant of the true facts, stand firm to my post, while the wind and the rain beat upon me, always expecting Coll's shout to pull my rope. Now the young sailor with one eye steered; for the moment old M'Donald and Coll and Coll's servant lay upon the forecastle, looking sharp out for the harbor. It was necessary to carry much cloth in order to keep the vessel off the shore of Coll island, which made for violent plunging about the rough sea. At last, to the surprise of all, Coll spied the harbor of Lochiern and cried, 'Thank God, we are safe!' We then ran up till we were opposite it, and soon afterwards we got into it and cast anchor. Staring, and still I think unaware of our full danger past, I finally let fall my rope which I'd held to tightly so long, and my uselessness suddenly came upon me, along with the idea that if I had served, I had done it only in not pulling down my mast, which notion might have entertained me more some other time. I hurried toward the hold to find whether Sir Robert had borne the terror after his sickness. Mr. Joseph emerged from the hold, having earlier descended. I stopped before him as Coll joined us. Mr. Joseph informed us that Sir Robert had all this time been quiet and unconcerned. Going below in his faintness, he had lain down on one of the beds, and having got free from sickness, was satisfied. The truth was, I thought as I listened to Mr. Joseph, that he knew nothing of our real danger, but fearless and unconcerned, was deprived of the common horror we others had shared. When I questioned Mr. Joseph further, he said Sir Robert had said that as the tempest drove, so he shaped his own ways. So I went down, stumbling below with Coll, to visit my employer and friend, not yet knowing what I was about. Sir Robert was lying in that philosophic tranquillity I knew so well from other occasions, with a greyhound of Coll's at his back to warm him. He didn't trouble himself to rise to our approach, and I fell then to my trembling knees, so relieved to find him well, and said in a most foolish manner, 'I have determined that upon our return to England, I shall sail for America. Will you not accompany me, my lord?' Only the greyhound moved, his head athwart the hip of my old companion, then Sir Robert said to me, very sadly, 'No, my young sir, I must sail, as you know, into a universal America—that is, into the death of us all, into my oblivion; for I am grown too old now for the bodily passage. Yet I do thank you for this voyage.' We all went then, unto our slumber, with heavy hearts, awaiting the morning and the calmed sea, when we might disembark."

At other times I read the Bible, in the translation commissioned by King James, my finger moving slowly or rapidly on the page, as though I could feel the words of my mother's language, my mouth moving too, on those sentences as if on food.

I remember a day and a scene clearly. Nearby me, in the woodline cabin, there lay a small English grammar and smaller dictionary, both upon my father's toolbox. The toolbox, a silver and pearl rosary, and two languages were all my inheritance from my parents. I sat in a tall chair reading. Long before, I had learned the language of that book from my mother, but the language always retained a strangeness for me, even after several years on the island, as if the language were not rightfully mine, but something stolen. Again, on the ship, I rediscovered the Bible in my mother's native tongue, which always partially revealed a new world to me. I was reading the first part of Genesis when the captain entered.

Hiram Wilson wasn't much like his older brother, Sir Robert. On sight, no one would have taken them for relations. I looked up at him absently, my finger hesitating on a word, and Wilson asked me to read to him, speaking to me in German, as he often did; so I read the first verses, huddling some words rapidly, slowly isolating others, my voice in tension, for some reason overexcited, as though anticipating an eminent revelation in the words I read or in my own voice.

The captain said I had a talent for languages, and I denied it. He had begun to speak only in English, the language I now believed was my own, possessing it for the continuance of my own life. And, as Captain Wilson read, I listened jealously, my eyes on his mouth, to words about the first parents, as the ship, intruding on rougher weather, continued to rock me, more erratically now. I was awash with the words Wilson read then from the story: in the captain's voice I heard the voices of a world I hadn't suspected before the voices; in those voices the hint of a single voice which could transform them all. At that time I felt I was about to hear the voice of God, speaking off the shore of America, in democratic accents, in the language of my mother.

Later, on deck, I waited eagerly for our landing, and my heart became frightened, thudding suddenly as though out of my control, and I dropped, accidentally, my mother's pearl and silver rosary, which I'd been clutching, into the sea. I had stopped crying when the captain joined me at the rail to speak of Pacific islands where natives said a hermaphroditic ocean, many males and females coupled in the single watery crea-ture, gave birth to boy and girl twins, the first land-people; and, as the long sea voyage ended, I grew yet more frightened, till the green-gray sea, under a bowl lined with heavy wool-like whorls, reflected nothing but this curdled, chambered sky, and, growing furious on its surface with white spume, tossed me up, like a sea vine, onto the Yorktown shore.

We said, "*February eighteenth, 1779,* we arrive early at the Little Wabash, actually two streams, five miles from the heights of one stream to the heights of the other, now the whole under water, generally about three feet deep, we send ahead two of our red men, Dove and Raven, both Piankeshaws, muddy-looking as this water as earth and sky now, we send them to reconnoiter the water, looking for land, this after incredible difficulties in the march, surpassing anything that any of us have ever experienced, we set to making a canoe, we camp on a height when the Indians find a piece of muddy land sticking out of the water, we amuse ourselves while Colonel Clark sits above us on a rise, he stares over the sheet of water, he shouts down to us that crossing over is but a diversion not to be taken seriously by men such as we, he laughs down at us but we, though we have often waded farther through water, seldom have above the range of half-leg deep, we are afraid our mission will not succeed, that there is no use to cross, we are much cast down and forlorn yet reluctant to return after all, so near now to St. Vincents, retreating through those difficulties we have so far endured, we hope the weather will freeze for us now, the ice to bear us safely over.

"*February nineteenth, 1779,* our piroque is completed, we man it and send it to explore the drowned lands on the opposite side of the Little Wabash, we find one spot of dry land of about half an acre, from thence back to the camp we mark the trees to guide us, the water high on the trunks, the colonel instructs the half-breed interpreter Drake to speak to us a story of the tribes which we often hear from him of an evening, so we are entertained but unconsoled.

"*February twentieth, 1779,* warm moist day for the season, our good fortune, this channel of the river about thirty yards wide, we build us a scaffold on the opposite side, which shore is three feet under water, the channel much deeper, we ferry our baggage over to the scaffold, by which time we all have crossed, proceeding with the sickly in our vessel, requiring several trips for them, passing from the half acre spied before we cross the smaller branch this day also, going by the marks upon the trees above the water level, as tracks cannot be seen because the water is too deep all places of our passage, we are not so discouraged, many comical diversions such as the little antic drummer who floated on his drum, all this greatly encouraging though our flesh is weakened, and we really begin to think ourselves, accomplishing this day, superior to other men, neither rivers nor seasons stopping our progress, we speak of what we will do to the enemy, seeing the main Wabash ahead a paltry creek only, as the colonel has said, and we make no doubt such men as we are can find a way to cross such a little water, as we see it, and we wind ourselves to such a pitch that we soon take St. Vincents, allegorically, we divide up the spoil, and before bedtime are far advanced on our route to Detroit, deep in Lake Indian country, so we are camped for the night, Colonel Clark nearby us past the campfire laughing heartily at our tales and jests, tonight we do not need Drake to entertain us, the colonel seeming so pleased with us, now there is no possibility of our retreat, having crossed these wide waters, should our enemy discover and overpower us, except by means of our galley if we should happen to meet with her, gay happy spirits we are though despite our unredeemable position and that our canoe has got lost, Colonel Clark saying we will steal vessels from houses opposite the town, we flatter ourselves all will be well with us now we are so close, we have orders not to fire any guns for the future but in case of great need."

After a year of wandering—trading my skills in wood and metal for food and shelter, in city, town, village, among the small clearings carved in the valleys of the eastern slope—as yet reluctant to begin an American life in any one place, I passed over the mountains, through great almost unpeopled forests, and descended to rolling hills, perennially blue-green, and I came to the Ohio and Corn Island.

It was at mid-afternoon that I landed in a piroque or canoe with three young men I'd met the night before, my father's heavy oak toolbox beside me in the boat.

Coming ashore, while still out on the water, I saw, for the first time, Orcus Berrigan, at the inlet, who seemed as huge and elemental, almost tusked, as an elephant. He lumbered into the river, naked, feeling the water at first with only his toes, then he walked confidently in until his head disappeared beneath the water, only to reemerge suddenly, as though his whole body, bobbing up, reappeared simultaneously in all its parts, and his body floated gently to shore, white on the blue water.

The first night on the island, Cantrell appeared as a poker player who teased me viciously about my age, Cantrell who was twenty-four. I wondered how I had provoked him.

Later, two men, who I learned the next day were Smith and Thomson, rolled about wrestling in darkness on the sandy shore, their naked bodies greased for the combat, near where Berrigan had gone down and reappeared. Whatever they did—perhaps singing, perhaps standing the careless guard—it seems to me they were like puppies then; that they were, on the island, endearingly as puppies, not quite men, yet unable to live without men to own them, preferring, in the absence of men like Colonel Clark or Sergeant Berrigan, doglike leaders, foxy like Cantrell, adoring for a time whoever would try to master them as they would have liked to master someone, finally resenting all their leaders, finding in infidelity their most human quality, puppies about to go spiteful, resentful: they were like men in false tails, the two together like something unlucky which has missed its chance to be transformed.

On the limestone rock, lying with the Indian woman who had come to me after all, I remembered or believed that I had been like a dog-boy among them, because I'd had to sleep, like some other boy, in their kennel, among the many young men who reminded me of Smith and Thomson. I thought my view of them unjust, but what could I do: it was the shape memory took on. I believed, at least until that belief also became confused, that Cantrell had been like a wild doggish animal, once tamed, now broken out again—a childish creature, perhaps born of a foxy father and henlike mother, resenting all other worlds.

Sometimes, on that island, waiting impatiently to depart, I'd felt mad and like a dog myself, and believed I'd been then another boy who, each day, guided us unnoticeably, leading us out to scamper, be combed, be brushed with long clusters of straw, to feed in the grassy meadow. I believed I'd felt that if this exercise was neglected, all of us might become irreversibly Smith and Thomson, potentially villainous pioneers, mothers and fathers of ourselves: I feared we'd get daughters and sons on wolf bitches running the shore of the river. Waiting on the island, my heart and business had got to be with the hounds, men I'd hoped to transform as if from another existence of myself, which I dreamt in silent attendance, hoping we would become kindly mature animals, something like men, hateful only to the evil in ourselves. All my images of the island became so distorted by later events; the lie asserted itself over the past until I began to lie about the island, believing memory's lying account.

It was still true that Colonel Clark moved among his men, a tall figure, blue-eyed, with reddish hair; at twenty-six he looked, it was rumored, like a younger Washington. He was then our definite leader, his voice casual in long periods, perplexing, as he spoke to us, in firelight nightly, of liberty and slavery, and of the fires burning for men.

The wait on the island had been long when, on June 26, 1778, we shot the Ohio falls, as light became darkness in a total eclipse of the sun, oars rhythmic like the evident fear in every back.

Beside the spring with Marie, Sawpootway, I recalled, as I had in the sun darkened behind the moon, most clearly after all, Clark talking; the mass of young dog-men; Cantrell tensed above the cards and coins; Berrigan's smooth flesh descent and abrupt resurgence, his white float to shore in the ruffled inlet.

She was with me when I

woke, older than I'd thought she was, more experienced to my inexperience in the initial difficulties. Her body was harder than I'd imagined, strangely flat, especially in the wide-boned pelvis. Her figure seemed very wide, with little depth. Even her breasts, though wide and round, splayed out on her reclining body.

I was a long time enjoying her, but when I was through, she continued clutching, in short thrusts. Then I felt very far from myself, as we lay beside each other on the limestone rock, as she trailed water across her body, dangling her hand into the spring, raising the hand to drip over the brown flesh and wide bones.

She began to talk in English—sometimes faulted badly, sometimes almost perfect, as if she were two women—telling me stories I understood to be her dreams. She said, when I asked her, that she'd learned the language as a parrot learns, that there was no wonder in her ability.

I asked, "Who did you learn it from?"

She said she didn't learn it from her husband. She turned away and said she'd learned it to defy him with another man. Then I thought she slept.

She turned toward me again, and said of Berrigan that he was large and kindly, protective.

I said, "Yes, he has protected me."

She said Berrigan had the power of healing and of death. She said his strength had lain in his arms and loins, which was the reason he could walk upright; but she said his head had once been very weak, like an eggshell.

She said she had seen the large and kindly man lick an egg which became a tiny man-like child. It was in winter, and the egg had hatched prematurely, in the mouth of a lustful Berrigan.

She said she had seen him before the birth, working upon a bear-woman whose face was hidden from her. She said they had made love as humans do. When the bear-woman had conceived, Berrigan took to a separate bed, a wall of the deep cave between him and the woman, respecting her privacy.

The bear-woman had given birth to a white pulp, terrible because eyeless. The bear-woman held it to her heart to draw its animal spirits up. She had become sleepy, but she held the pulp of the child for fourteen days before she went away by herself to sleep for three months. Berrigan had then made the egg from which the bear-child, tiny man, hatched.

Berrigan came from the cave and staggered, blinded beneath the sun. He found some honey for the child and himself. Later, when the child was grown, the bear-man ate a thick, swollen root and seemed to die.

The newest Berrigan, after the seeming death, was a buffalo-man, pursued, by hunting hounds run by Smith and Thomson.

I said, "Animals aren't really men."

She said that Berrigan released fiery excrement, large like him: the prairie caught fire, then the forest, a flaming wall of trees, cutting off his pursuers.

She said that animals are really men, and I shrugged, unconvinced.

I said, "Talk to me about yourself."

She said she could remember her childhood clearly. She remembered her father who sucked snakes from their holes with his nostrils, when she and her mother were very hungry and ill on the plains in the winters. After they feasted on the rattlesnakes, her father pretended to remove the skins of wife and daughter with a small stone knife. He sang then as they carefully listened.

She said her parents were both concupiscent, that she inherited a constant need for sex from them.

She said her name meant girl-fawn or antelope-child, which meant to hide or to make a sign.

She said that when they traveled to new feeding grounds, after the buffalo, the tribe crossed the more difficult rivers single file, heads on preceding haunches, with her father, the shaman, leading them, their chief hanging on, like a short fish's tail, at the end of the tribal column, the dogs and horses crossing on their own.

She said that her father was now two hundred years old, that he looked like a small boy because he'd eaten his tribesmen, so much of their flesh, poisoning them, to become immortal: the last person he'd eaten had been her mother; the girl, Sawpootway, frightened, soon found a way to escape from her people, though she hadn't sought the opportunity.

She said she remembered her birth, how her parents had hid her, tenderly, carefully, in chokecherry bushes, how they stamped their feet, jutted their white-painted buttocks, and said to keep hidden, only to discover her, as if in surprised pleasure, very soon after her hiding, pretending they'd never seen her before, making believe she was someone else's child mysteriously delivered to them, their own child given to them like a present.

I no longer understood her tales to be from her dreams. I asked, "What of Smith and Thomson?"

She said that men are really animals. She spoke sharply. She said that Smith and Thomson's parents were married by chance. She said they would mate with panther-bitches which will bear faceless twins, meaner versions of themselves, able to escape from lions only to be destroyed, with a strange beast and in another life, by the buffalo.

I said, "I think you're right. I've thought of something like that myself."

She asked me if I really believed her.

"Yes," I said, "I've seen the same thing."

She moved her face close to mine, and she laughed at me.

She seemed to have become impatient, after laughing, and she slid into the water. The water rose to her waist.

I leaned down from the limestone, and asked, "But what of me, how have you seen me?"

She said I was like a man who would be held up, as young eagles are held, to the sun, that if I gazed fearlessly, with uninjured power, while the light burned away obscuring membranes from the surfaces of my eyes, my god might be revealed to me.

She slid her wide, depthless body beneath the spring's current, crouching there, and the water cascaded from her loose hair when she stood again. She seemed even more impatient, and said that she must go to her husband who lay under a deerskin.

"No," I said, "you don't have to leave yet. He'll still be sleeping."

She smiled up at me, condescendingly, and pulled her body onto the ledge.

I said, "Tell me more about yourself."

Unsmiling, she became more nervous. She said that she had been an Indian girl, but that she would really be a white woman now.

I felt the sex and talk had left me far away from myself, like an animal out of his natural element; though I remained intensely aware of everything that was said or that happened. "Stay," I said.

She said, "I must come back to Orcus Berrigan

now." She pronounced the words distinctly, with attention to the individual sounds.

I didn't argue; but before she could go, when we'd dressed ourselves, Berrigan appeared through the trees, his once full beard trimmed neatly, wispish at his chin, his features seeming larger, emerging from the hair he'd had before.

Smith and Thomson were dead, he told us, also the Frenchman, Jacques LeGuey. Berrigan said they had attacked him, circling with knives, after Sawpootway had left him. He said, "It must have been the gold. Then that half-breed came, and he couldn't have come a better time. I can't think what it was, if it wasn't the gold they wanted." He looked at Marie and blushed.

In a deep voice, Marie said it was what men deserved of each other.

Berrigan said that he and the Indian had killed them. He said to come see them, he said, crying. He fell onto all fours, fell to pounding the rock. He bellowed above the spring, beneath the white sycamores.

Behind Berrigan, winding through the wood, appeared a pig-tailed Indian man, the half-breed Drake. I recognized him immediately, Clark's interpreter, naked above his waist, in white man's breeches, the beak-nosed man, riding a gray mule, the long-eared mule without reins or saddle, only the breeches and a patterned blanket between them, between man and animal. I recognized Drake, and was afraid, as if Cantrell's thin face had appeared before my eyes.

When we came to view the bodies, Berrigan stood behind Marie and me, stroking the new wisp of his beard, two shovels tucked under his arm. I looked around once quickly, took a shovel, and began to dig in the clearing. Marie shuddered, as though she would shrug her skin off, surrounded as she was by the corpses, on the small rise of the ground, where Berrigan and the Indian, Drake, had fought. The Indian and his gray-white, his blue mule watched all from the clearing's edge, casually, as though he were through with all of us now, as though the previous fight and present scene had become unimportant.

Marie spoke angrily, in French, to the dead Jacques LeGuey. He lay alone, seeming, from a distance, as casual as the Indian and mule, almost smiling in his death, on the southern side of the mound. A small fire had gone out nearby him.

Smith and Thomson had fallen separately, cut off from each other by the rise of ground, their bodies a smoky gray, fanged gaping mouths and emptied eyes in the slightly bloody heads, as in my vision of their evil—wolf-hounds fallen, their long, lean bellies no longer pulsing outward at the sides, in their lives.

Digging rapidly, I couldn't help peeking, now and then, at the dead figures, once so full of playful animal or human life. Jacques, alone of the three, appeared to have returned to a primary state, into a world where he belonged: he seemed shriveled in death, carefully dried like an animal skin, as if all his water had withdrawn from him, poured out, so he looked ancient, artificially preserved, somehow more human dead, or at least more elementary, than he had in life, now seeming wise, returning naturally to his own world.

The three lay, in a limp relation to death, among large jagged fragments of wine jugs and among whole knives. On a closer view, the bodies of Smith and Thomson, though not LeGuey's marred but formal body, lay as if their spines had been snapped under great pressure. I saw only minimal blood: all three scalps were missing large clumps of hair, patchy, as though the heads had been pecked, hair plucked out like feathers, as though one bird had destroyed others; and Jacques, dirtied, disheveled, seemed to have been trampled—into that primary, original condition.

There was little blood visible, only on the heads, but when we lifted Jacques, I discovered the back of his skull crushed as if with a hoof; blood was there enough, matted with bear grease in his dark, thin hair. Marie saw the blood and began to curse him again.

For the moment, our scene of death, the surround of corpses, became unbearable to me, and I snapped, "Shuttup!"

She began to scream at me. She said that her husband had betrayed her by dying, that it was what men did, betray their women, for fear women were more powerful than them. I started to wrap the deerskin around Jacques, but she jerked the skin away in anger.

Berrigan, snorting, often using his hands, worked at the second, much larger grave, and Marie joined him, while I, more and more angry with everything, rolled Jacques onto the skin, wrapped the dead man, worked his light body into the grave I'd dug, and threw in a handful of dirt, which landed on the wizened face. I thought of words spoken in Latin at my father's grave. Hurriedly, forgetting, I shoveled earth back into the hole, earth into earth: Jacques, even Smith and Thomson, would assume the rhythms of this earth.

Marie kept putting her hands on Berrigan, but he ignored her touch. She was sitting down, crying, watching Berrigan finish the double grave.

Berrigan and I dragged Smith and Thomson by the legs, and tumbled them down into a heap, tangled upon each other, holding each other down. Berrigan sighed deeply, and I wiped my hands on myself: the worst was over.

I'd forgotten about the Indian and the mule behind us, as though they didn't matter, as though all that mattered was the correct placement of corpses, small dead animals placed, as though Cantrell would not be close to us if this half-breed was who, here and now, seemed suddenly surprising. The attention Drake had paid Berrigan and me during the march to Vincennes took on a different significance in his new presence. I wondered if he'd followed us, but couldn't imagine why he would.

I looked at the thin, burned-out sticks of wood, of the fire Berrigan had made to keep him and Sawpootway warm when they'd been naked. I felt uneasy, and tried to concentrate only on what I was doing, the thrust of my shovel, the lift of transition and heave of unloading, my repetitious occupation, as if that would steady me. I couldn't concentrate, trying so hard, though I had done it naturally in a time before I remembered the Indian and the mule.

I heard Marie whimpering at my back. As we covered the bodies, she began to talk rapidly, as if avid to release herself from the scene, addressing Berrigan's rising and falling back. She said that LeGuey had taken her from her people. She said that Berrigan had taken her from LeGuey. Where would Berrigan take her now? Just what did Berrigan intend to do with her, now he'd got her? She was his. What was his idea?

I looked at her and she was still weeping, trembling more intensely, looking thinner. I returned to my work and she said that Jacques had taken two wives, then become frightened, of nothing, and fled, bearing his favorite wife, the one he loved, Sawpootway, in his arms, the other, the wife he despised, on his back. She said she was the loved girl, and for many miles Jacques bore her safely before him, while the hated one desperately clung, with arms and legs, to his extended neck and heaving sides, in great fear LeGuey would let her fall from his back. This hated one always urged him on, faster and faster. At last the runner became too tired to carry both women. Terrified to pause, he threw the loved wife aside, to run on all fours, as if in his natural posture, easily bearing the despised woman to safety.

We'd finished our work and, leaning side by side on the shovels, we listened carefully as she concluded her story, Berrigan glancing at me as if to see if I heard what he did; I nodded to say I heard it too. Drake and the mule just watched us as before. Marie, her skin drained white, rose and threw herself face down on Jacques's grave. Slowly, she stroked wide arcs, moved her legs and arms back and forth, smoothing the freshly turned earth between her and Jacques.

When she became still, we couldn't wake her. Drake moved then, and he would have placed her across the long-eared bluish mule, but Berrigan wrapped her in his arms and carried her through the full trees and the tree stumps into the cabin, and he laid her apparently lifeless body in the rag-piled corner, as if he were proud of her, his eyes slightly glazed, as with horn, as if she'd bewitched him.

I went back outside, where Drake stood with his mule between two stumps. I said, "Did you follow us?"

In a moment he said, staring through the open cabin door, "I heard her name, and I knew who she was. She didn't know me ever. She was too young. But I didn't know there would be this connection. I . . ."

For a time his lips continued to move, but I heard none of his words. He didn't seem to be answering my question, so I tried again when the lips stopped moving. I asked him, "Did you see Cantrell?"

From the way he looked, I knew he thought he'd said too much already. He closed his eyes, and turned toward his mule. They went together toward some long dry grass put up in a kind of rick.

I walked back to the limestone shelf and the creek by myself, dazed by events. I felt so torn away, like a page from a book, a division in me. I was so tired, dreamed on the ledge without sleeping, imagined an unwished future as if it were my detailed past, saw what I wouldn't wish to remember, my will borne away from me in images of my own death, as though on a current I could initiate but couldn't control long. It seemed I remembered myself, as if someone else spoke in quotation of me, beyond my death, like another voice above the stream, one too much like my own—though I heard nothing but the movement of the water, animals scurrying, some birdsong—as if I, or someone like me, spoke as I almost slept, imagining my death, after the other deaths; yet it was, I knew, my own voice as if mirrored in echo, recurring to me from the imagined future, reflected back across the imaginary event, this voice of mine as if it weren't my voice, this voice after the voice began with which we once spoke of the water journey, preceding the voices I'll hear again almost too soon now. I became aware of a vision spread on my eyes like a film, and of my deep pulse just to the front of my ears. Perhaps, after all, I did sleep, troubled by a dream of myself, while Berrigan hammered in the clearing, mending wheels on the trapper's wagon, steadying the axles, shoring up the seat and sideboards, performing work in which I was skilled.

I said, "It had all hurt: the young bodies lying in the burning house, while my grandsons, from the yard, watched what they'd done, as I rode up too late from the town and lawyer; our flight from the broad river, northwest into the first hills, the crackling afternoon, the soft cold winter night, the fragile morning; the death of my two young grandsons, their crisp bodies lying lead-heavy in the snow, below the old man I was, in the snow-speckled ravine, their chests minutely spotted with blood, as the old, now familiar sun rose higher and broke again from cloud cover, orange in its core, blue-fringed, my grandsons, Jesus and Pedro, my Pedro's sons, dead in the white hills above the crossing, lying on their backs, fully clothed, only their features appearing—scarcely formed yet from the dark faces, just boys, their white and black eyes outstanding—and their dark cupped hands, in the shape of claws, my grandsons who'd slain the man Caldwell's sons, my grandsons fallen now to Caldwell and his mob; the humiliation of my nakedness before such men, while the vigilantes nudged each other, laughing behind the severe countenance of Caldwell, who bore his saber in one hand, a leather bag in the other, who spoke to me, the old man, for the first time ever, for I'd never seen him before, never heard of him before yesterday, who claimed he'd bought the land from a grandson I didn't know I even had, this Emerson Caldwell saying, 'This for Paris and Ulysses, for *my* land,' speaking names strange in this place, as he stood beside the lawyer who I did remember and who couldn't seem to quit talking, not quite yet, saying over and over again to Caldwell or to me that if either of us or both had let things be settled in the courts, this needn't have happened to us, but he didn't understand what would happen next, and he talked as if the four dead boys, who'd quarreled, would have understood him—the two now buried who died in the house, and my two who'd shot them and burned down the house—and I

looked at my grandsons dead in the clearing, in the ravine, spotted with blood as if sparrows had pecked
briefly at their chests trying to feed; the dull saber
which Caldwell, whose face now resembled the almost human face of a beaver, worked between my old
thighs, sawing or hacking, something you wouldn't
believe would happen until it did, while the lawyer
and I screamed as if we were a single person, while
some of the men did turn away though they wouldn't
interfere or depart, none of them, while Caldwell—
holding the leather pouch open, drawstring flush
against the top of the leather, the waiting pouch—
knelt and mumbled about the end of generations,
Caldwell who'd found his gunshot, burned sons, the
extinguished faces—as though, in them, fire had overcome water—and identified them by clothing and
location, in the smoldering house that had been mine;
and at last the mortal rush of blood as my members
fell into the pouch, so they had to prop me quickly on
the gray horse, to hang me before I died on them, as
I felt somewhere other than my death or life, listened
to myself, to my dying body—a world within the
body, waving, between earth and sky in the branches
—knew my own mind, conferred with my flesh, and
cried out for something as if it were lost—fire or
water—as the gray horse, whipped hard by Caldwell's
saber, plunged forward, knocking down a vigilante,
and slid over the ravine lip, disappearing northwestward through the white-capped hills: my death all
hurt me, and I lay behind the scene then, like an invisible sun, deep violet and rare, illuminating."

We said, "*February twenty-first,* 1779, we
hear, for first time, at break of this day Governor

Long's morning gun, we march through several deep runs, through rain and water, we see some fine land, we send our commissary with three other men to cross the river Embarrass if possible and to proceed to a plantation opposite Port St. Vincents in order to steal boats or canoes to ferry us across the Wabash, after about an hour by the sun we get near the Embarrass, find the country all overflown with waters, we strive to find the Wabash, we travel till eight o'clock in mud and water but we can find no place to encamp on, much grumbling, after some time the commissary returns with his party finding it impossible to cross Embarrass River, we find the water falling from a small spot of ground, stay there the remainder of the night, drizzly and dark weather, the men growing mutinous against Clark, we find a dog shot floating muddy in the water late in the night just as we begin to encamp.

"*February twenty-fourth,* 1779, we are at the Wabash, the Embarrass endured in difficulty, one company is set to make a canoe, four of our men return so wearied at three o'clock after spending their night on some old logs in the water, another company returns having discovered four large campfires about a league distant from our camp which seemed to them to be fires of Indians and whites, immediately Colonel Clark sends two men in the canoe down to meet our bateau with orders to come on day and night, that being our last hope and we starving, many of us are much cast down, grumbling against Clark, particularly our volunteers who now wish they had not come, no provisions of any sort now two days, hard fortune, Clark orders more canoes built, he is laughing at the fainthearted without attempting to persuade or dissuade them but tells us all he should be glad if we would go out and kill some deer, we going, we are confused with such conduct on his part, then he behaves as if there were no doubt of our success, laughing and saying that were we hungry there remained plenty of good horses.

"*February twenty-fifth, 1779,* our camp very quiet but hungry we almost despair, many of us, even regulars, talk of returning no matter the hardships, we fall to making more piroques when about twelve o'clock our sentry on the river brings to a boat with five Frenchmen from the post who tell us we are not as yet discovered as we have feared, the inhabitants are many well disposed to us and our cause and others indifferent to either side, the brother of one of our captains returns to us who with his brother formerly had been taken in the fort by accident on an expedition and says that one British party with a party of Indians are now seven days in pursuit of him as he eluded them deviously, that his brother is well and imprisoned with a friendly Indian, and he has much news other to our favor such as repairs done the fort and the strength of it, he also informs us of two canoes he'd set adrift in order to escape pursuit some distance above us and the colonel orders that a party go in search of them, they return late with one only, we kill a deer in a thicket, a fawn, throttling it where it lay crippled by some incident unknown to us, very acceptable eating."

Caldwell said, "I said, 'This for Paris and Ulysses, and for *my* land.' I believed it had been a question of the land I purchased from young Blue. The old man might not have been Gerhard Blau after all, screaming silently. He was almost dead anyway, too old to live in the world; his flesh

was dead. He looked more like a Mexican or an Indian. If it was his land he shouldn't have stayed away so long, till everyone forgot him. And his son came up from New Orleans with that new wife and said his father was dead and changed their name. And I had never seen his father, and the grandson sold it.

"I said, 'No more generations!' I muttered, hacking through, and the blood gushed under the dull edge, the torrent spurting into my mouth before I could close it, as the old man's screams, high-pitched, became audible again. I bought it so my sons would have something to do, something more. I spat out the blood, swallowing some against my will, then intentionally let saber fall, and pulled the drawstrings tight on the pouch.

"A gray horse was brought up, and two men propped the old man up in the saddle. I slapped the horse with the bloody flat side of my saber, as the noose and length of rope sprung the old man toward the branches, and the old man's blood rained down on those below him, patterning the earth, and the men dodged back from his swinging path, dodging his blood.

"Two men dug a hole behind the cottonwood with short knives, and the old man, whoever he was, no longer swinging, was brought down. Other men began, on my orders, to carve small, scattered holes in the earth. The lawyer sat weeping, his back turned from the scene over near some scrub pine, while the biggest man among us received the saber from me, and in strong, sudden strokes, sliced the body into parts, so I would be revenged on the body.

"When the big man finished—breaking the ankle bones and wrist bones, cutting off the feet and hands from severed limbs—I, who'd tied the pouch tight to my waist, distributed the blood-drained pieces, like remnants of a god who, if whole, I feared would rise to take revenge, scattered the body among the little holes in the narrow bare ravine.

"I left the grandsons, who Hastings says were named Jesus and Pedro, lying as they'd fallen, for scavengers to eat, hunkered birds I could foresee on that earth, destroying progeny, a spectacle upon the winter ground, like the pattern of blood the old man left behind when he swung, visible bodies and pattern like signature or relics of a faded world, as though they were significant members of a vanished, alien body."

We said, "*February twenty-sixth, 1779,* at break of day we begin to ferry our men over in two canoes to a small hill called the Momib or Bubbriss, three men go to look for a passage shallow enough and are discovered to two men in a canoe but cannot fetch the strangers to, the whole army being over we think to get near to town this night, we plunge into the water sometimes to the neck for more than one league when we stop on the next hill of the same name, no dry land on any side for many leagues, we cannot get along farther, it seems impossible, we encamp, rain all this day too, no provisions, Colonel Clark returns in a canoe, we see him speak seriously to one of his officers, the whole of us alarmed without knowing what he says, we run from one to another bewailing our situation, Clark views our confusion, he whispers to his officers for a moment, putting water in a major's hand, he pours on powder very black, darkens the major's face, gives a warwhoop Indian fashion, and marches himself into the water, we gaze and fall in astonished, one after another without saying a word, a favorite song beginning near the front and passing back is taken up by us throughout the line of our march and the whole of us go on as cheerfully as ever men did under such circumstances, one of our men discovers a path under the water which keeps to the highest ground, a path being easily discoverable with the feet under water facilitating our passage.

"*February twenty-seventh*, 1779, Colonel Clark encourages us which gives us great spirit, we march on in the waters, those that are weak and famished from so much fatigue and fasting ride horseback or go in the canoes, we come on a league farther to some sugar camps, where we remain the night through, we hear the evening and morning guns from the fort, as we don't even see any fish no provisions yet, Lord help us."

Cantrell said, "I despised my
men, pretending to love them. I felt I lowered myself to them, pretending the dissimilar men were my equals. They believed me and obeyed me. I was reluctant to leave them, to lose control: in departure I bore a message, obtained from Clark, for the fort at Kaskaskia. I wasn't a deserter.

"I headed the gray mare west on the prairie, without any of my men, pursuing the cold trail I knew would lead straight to the gold. Whenever I was alone with myself as I was on the mare, or in acute tenderness with a woman, or in my wrath with a man, then I felt my life spurt up my body, molten sap dazzling at my points, like the tight green buds on the prairie trees around me, flared at my extremities— toes, genitals, fingers, nose, eyes, ears, tongue—thin, feathery tentacles of fire, hard and tight against their near future life, balled up and feeling out the world I continually, unwillingly entered, the world which entered me. I was alive within myself as if the world—of hate or love, or simple loneliness and envy—were budding, not quite yet in explosion, to manifest itself, reveal its secret coils through me, earth's intricate corridors and walled gardens.

"For all my foxy nature and sudden, cocky passions, I hadn't learned my partners had left with the boy till the next afternoon. Discipline was lax at the fort after the troubling passage through the Illinois, as Clark worked furiously to obtain from the distant authorities men and supplies for an assault on Detroit, while the men roved heedlessly about the town and fort, disappearing for days and nights, after game as if they weren't a kind of game themselves, their constant squirrely chatter contradicting itself, their sluggish life which could break so erratically into negation or negative affirmations, living in their bodies as if in the surfaces of mirrors, as if their bodies were only reflections of their minds, never bodies but just the paltry reflection of bodies the mind reveals; so they didn't seem to be alive at all, in any truly physical sense, remaining at last mindless and dwelling only in their divided, ununited bodies, nothing but trivial senses after all. Yet I was glad they weren't alive as I was, for my power over them lay, I knew, in their very unreality and in the thin, hard, potentially explosive ego I clung to, almost bursting against their mirrored world, ego almost leaping into full leaves or flowers: when I led them the men lived, I believed, in their surface reflections in my eyes, as if I were their body.

"I moved my horse across the prairie world, nearing the Kaskaskia River, myself a small world of the budlike ego struggling as if down a branch, along the invisible trail of those I pursued, expecting to explode on arrival at the roots, a cannibal bloom devouring the real earth, beyond all mirrors. And I hadn't willingly deserted the place I'd founded on the tree, but now—forced to move by the betrayal of my partners, who I'd led victoriously against the escaped British wagon—I repeated the route my betrayers had taken, generally, with my own variations: I traveled only a day behind them, encountered the swamp and drizzle, the refrozen earth, the long hanks of snow falling down, the glassy fragility of the frozen prairie, and the warming successive days; yet I traveled without their visions of myself, or of gold, or of dark women, or of young girls swinging in tree branches while hawks hummed through circling air around her head.

"My body and mind were willfully concentrated on vengeance, slavishly, not merely to even up the score, but to end the domination of others over me, forever removing the causes of envy's bite. I became indifferent to my own two troopers, Smith and Thomson, who I would simply and quickly kill, returning them to the earth from which they could never rise again, who would belong simply to the elemental earth: I would slay them indifferently, as the farmer destroys egg-sucking hounds, and I would let them dissolve forever into the earth, to which they forever belonged: they would need no weight but their own to bear them down, no dissolution but their own living dissolution to reduce them.

"My concern was with the other two men. I felt a peculiarly strong desire to kill the German boy, Blau, and had visions of the others, once the younger one was dead, falling consequently like domino tiles in a line, in my resentful dream, as the boy fell, as the earth uncoiled its bowels for the gift of a human life, like a snake with her brood of Smiths and Thomsons rending his body, drinking his steaming blood, swallowing the tender pieces slowly to prolong the feast, the boy unnaturally pinned to the serpent's belly, aspiring to rise but unable through the serpentine tangles.

"Yet, strangely, as I neared the trapper's cabin, I wished to be beyond the bud, beyond the implications of my vision, free of my envy of the boy, of the giant Berrigan—who might fight, as earth's near equal, against his reduction to earth, but might easily fall when the boy fell—to feel, simply, in seizures of the momentary life, the tenuous flames at the tips of my fingers, to hear, through my opening fires, the fetid slap of waters at recumbent shores; but I always willed the envy to return, my ancient resentment which, from someplace in myself, continually rose up again, bodily, I felt, as if resurrected, its eyes like long swords, its tongue of fine metal, creating a discord my will persistently moved through.

"In the woods I discovered the clearing of fresh, unmarked graves, and I found the shovels. I dug hastily to find out who lay buried, afraid I'd find Blau and Berrigan, but secretly almost hoping I'd find a release from my willful revenge in finding them. I studied the bodies of the men Berrigan and Drake had killed. I wondered at my troopers' tangled rootlike bodies. I was surprised that the trapper, LeGuey, was dead, and I searched for the Indian woman, thinking she might be hiding somewhere.

"Then I realized the trapper's old wagon was gone, and I shoveled the earth back onto the corpses, tamped the blanketing earth, damply black like embers of a drowned fire, and prodded the graves, finally, thoughtfully, with my toes; then I rode again, five miles through a gray world which was transfixed by lightning, stabbing golden pins, thunder like the many voices of quarreling gods, to discover the terrible, empty, dark mouth, in a windy river gully, from which the Indian Drake, Berrigan and Marie, and Blau had removed the gold bars, like teeth from an old woman's mouth. Under the storm, I was frightened; I leaned into the gray mare's side for protection, and shook, like a leaf or flower, in the hard rising wind off the river. My shoulder ached where my wound lay hidden. I saw a dark tree become suddenly white in my presence, and I knew their trail was lost."

Someone said, "The white-haired ferryman managed the route carefully, with ease, altering the drift only slightly with the guideline, pulling the travelers through the soft arch toward the opposing shore downstream. The river was high but not rough in the lee of the island, full of debris—branches, canoes, and other floating or submerged stuff less easily identified—of its full, broad life in the spring, pouring south, eating into its own distance. The water had been higher. The island was cluttered, emerging as the river fell aside, increasing in land, white like a polar bear stranded, coming clean beneath its crowned head of river waste.

"The unbusy dark he-mule, on the approaching western bank, cropped the new grass at his planted hoofs, before Ste. Genevieve in the evening sunlight, as the raft, with its burden of men and a woman, horses and she-mule (necks serpentine over the side rails) used the river's current to fall toward the Spanish shore.

"The Indian Drake sat on the wagon seat alone, his beaklike nose illuminated in the setting sun, while Gerhard, wrapped in the trapper's pile of furs which covered the gold, felt cold or feverish in sleep, though his eyes were staring open. He was apparently abstracted from the scene as if he needed other eyes to see it by.

"Marie and Berrigan leaned together at the stern rail, peering into the darkness gathered on the eastern shore, darkness divided by lightning demonstrated in thunder rolls. They turned away, unable to see the damp gully from which Cantrell would turn toward the Kaskaskia fort, giving up, not his vengeance, but the particular object and trail.

"The river was another animal. Now even the island didn't seem to really exist within it. Both river banks, though the height of flood was past, appeared to recede; even the bank they approached diminished like the sun above it. The passengers felt tugs and pulls upon them, back and forth as if they were tide-bound objects, debris of the river, and they advanced as though only because the sun, in its sinking, had assumed a power of tide upon the river stronger than the hold of the gray, shattered sky and land behind, than the pull of the gully with its terrible mouth, the funeral clearing, the stumps about the cabin, other sun-receded things, stronger than the force Cantrell, who'd fallen by his horse, exerted on them. They didn't appear to approach things which had been diminished in them, only another shore, slightly sunlit, contrasting with the eastern in sundown opposed to storm. They were all aware, even the animals, of the shore behind, lightning scarred, a panicked landscape like terrible flashes of insight and terrible rumbling voices of gods who had died in the travelers, as though still-born.

"The river was another animal country than either shore, an interim, casual through power, as if for the moment a caress was allowed, a relaxation of tensions, a pause of tongues reclining in the mouths, while in the body of the Mississippi, beneath the ferry route, large-eyed fish swam unconcerned, at one with the current; as though in wafted, tropical air a man and woman, breathing out and breathing in, had learned to take for granted the simplest aspect of themselves, natural alternation in themselves of a conjugal life they no longer were willing to worry about, as if they waited, patiently, for a child to wake up, before a journey."

Two

We said, "*February twenty-eighth,* 1779, we set off to cross the plain called Horseshoe Plain, about four miles long, all covered with water breast high, this after the coldest night we have had, our earlier passages in weather warm and moist, here we expect some of us will perish, having got froze in the night, and so long fasting, ice in the water one half to three quarters of an inch thick near the shores and in still water, but the morning after the finest we have had on our march, we have no other recourse but wading this plain or rather lake of waters, we walk at the entry, without food, benumbed with cold, up to our waists in water covered with broken ice, we balk and retreat, huddling down to warm ourselves together as best we can, we relight the fires, Colonel Clark speaks to us calmly a long time, reminding us of our desire to reach the fort, to see our cause accomplished, how our fatigue and hunger will disappear in the opposite woods, of our victory and revenge on the British, on Governor Long the Hair-buyer, for setting savages to pillage our back settlements, set on our families, the women and children of others reminding us of our own future wives and inheritors, at which speech our spirits revive somewhat and we prepare to try the water again, extinguishing the renewed campfires, still we hold back until Colonel Clark mounts our small drummer on the back of a sergeant, more than six feet in his stockings, stout, athletic, devoted to the colonel, who orders him to plunge into the icy waters, and he does so, the little jerky drummer mounted on the stalwart sergeant, beating out our *charge* from his lofty perch, while Clark with sword in hand follows them, giving the command while he throws aside the floating ice, crying out to us, 'Forward!'; we are elated and amused with this scene, we obey promptly and Clark, to command obedience from any still mutinous members, orders twenty-five men to our rear with orders to shoot anybody found to be retreating as he wishes to have, he says, no such person among us, we plunge ourselves into the water despite weakness from exercise and hunger, holding our rifles and powder above our heads, in spite of all obstacles we reach the high woods beyond us safely, the little canoes plying back and forth across the waters, conveying the sickly to shore while the more sturdy among us often bear our weaker brothers up, our comradeship so stubborn that we plunge straight on spiritedly on discovering no dry land in the woods we've seen the boats disappearing into, for the woods are a great advantage to the weak who cling to the trees and float on old logs until taken off by the canoes, so that many of us finally stumble ashore about one o'clock when we come in sight of the town, we halt on a small dry hill of land called Warren's island, many falling ashore with their bodies half in the water, not being able to support themselves without the flood, where we take a prisoner hunting ducks who informs us that no person suspects our coming at this season of the year out of the west overland, tonight Drake tells us a story and we do not need to tell each other we have won."

Drake said, "At the suggestion of Colonel Clark, I recite my half-breed tales to the half-breed whites, these modern renegades, the father-haters, mother-lovers, the almost-runaways, their mothers' missionaries in the campfire light, whose features are diffused, in flame, throughout the surrounding waters, these dippers of cane poles, fishmanglers, mouthing dogs, bark bark. I have only contempt for them and for myself, and I hate myself for obeying the colonel I don't love. I hate Raven and Dove, the colonel's other scouting birds, sent forward to find land, to guide these in-between creatures to the scenes of their violence. I find their accumulated, massive wills a terrible obstruction to any true story.

"Believing this fire, on the night of February eighth, is my fire, blooming through the watery prairie of my body, refracted through my mud-welling waters, in me becoming the fire of bitterness, through my long exile, of gall, not wrath or love, though I feel violent toward these men, hating my own mother with something of their own stubborn quality of will, reversing them in my body, while they sit in the circle, featureless in the pink, blooming night on the external waters, and I tell the story of a picture they don't understand, my voice edged with the yellow flames, the petals of bitterness and of self-hatred, knowing I am more like these men than I wish. Later, another night, I may entertain them.

"When I first try to see her, my ancestress, there are three ships in the harbor with red crosses on the white sails. After the water, the shoreline. A stiff, pointed fire on the beach. The log shelter, leafless, is next, supported by gnarled, large-bolled, forked trees, also leafless. A distorted monkey, possibly only an Indian child, hangs from the roof as if representing a stranger in the scene.

"The Indians themselves look European and are stiffly portrayed like the beach fire, mostly lifeless. Beneath the shelter two or three lovers enact concupiscence. One apparently embraces and kisses the other. A third leans on the kisser or gnaws her own forearm. It's difficult to be sure of anyone's sex, though all but one of them face me, inland, and they are dressed scantily in feathers or in stiff-spined leaves. It is as if the stubborn will of Clark were imposed upon the picture as on his men.

"I look at them from inside this country, inside this America, down centuries of my ancestry. The kisser-embracer appears to be male, his two companions females. The companion to my right has her hand on the lover's upper thigh. The one on my left, on the lover's right, appears to rest her elbow on his shoulder, leaning toward him. In general, the women seem to have longer hair than the men, briefer leaves or lengths of feather at their waists, more pendulant breasts.

"There is, beneath the initial stiffness, something female-voluptuous about the entire scene which I haven't described all of yet. Perhaps the ancestress I'm trying to see, in this first time, is none of the four probable-women, but some rather simple combination of the four, or just perhaps the scene in its soft undercurrent beneath the stiff imposition of the artist's will. Perhaps she, also an invisible guide, like me, watches the scene, say four distributions of herself among the Indian women, the hints of her sex in the figures of four males, at least three of whom the artist seems to have misunderstood, making them merely illustrative companions in the hunt.

"One of these three men, with his back turned to me, touches another. The third stands a little apart, toward the center, above a curly-haired boy-child. The group of three hunters occupies my right hand. The third has grown in importance, when I see him above the child.

"That child seems now the most masculine image since he's coupled with the warrior, the two of them so sturdy. There are only three children, unless I count that swinging monkey as one, and he is surely, if child of any woman, a bastard, idiot, silly fool, in the rafters of the lodge, too balmy for meaning.

"Approaching the center foreground, to my left of the central, bolled tree, just outside the shelter, stands the ignored, the fourth woman, a kind of observer apparently, back turned to me, watching from the left, leaves fanned very scarcely on her ass, as she holds the stalk of some plant. The plant might be corn, but is likely tobacco. Is this Pocahontas? Is this the girl or woman I've been looking for? Have I found her as her steady gaze carries through the flow of my imagined, painted scene, through the center of the bridal-lodge or funeral-pole, behind the mother, before the lovers, through the monkey-child, behind the warriors and the children, through the ships, in the upper right-hand corner, which diminish in size till the last ship rises smally from the horizon? Is this my ancestress, in the egg, the future Pocahontas, full or partial?

"The monkey-child hangs from one hand; his feet dangle, the limpest things in the scene, really dead feet as if severed and independently suspended from the roof. I assume he is male. His left hand or paw seems to point straight down toward the curly head of the eldest of the three children, the one beneath the elbow of the warrior. The creature's tail, if he has one, isn't visible. His ass faces the ships. The picture isn't in color either, so I couldn't tell any more about genitals or buttocks if I could see them.

"The boy-child below, the one person whose sex is beyond question though he appears less masculine now, seems unaware of the monkey-child's gesture toward him. He gazes past the center pole to a smaller, beseeching child directly in line beneath the lodge pole which largely, full of bolls and sawed-off limb stubs, dominates the center as it descends from the monkey on my right to the mother on my left. The pole barely divides the monkey and mother. The smallest child suckles her right breast while the curly-haired child watches.

"Here is the Indian mother sitting on two flat stones, from concupiscence, this mother sitting, seen through my guiding eyes, across my twinned blood. She does resemble a famous portrait of Pocahontas, but with feathers at her neck instead of the Jacobean ruff in which her husband disguised her.

"Perhaps Pocahontas is in the picture projecting her future through three children, the monkey-child as a possible fourth part restoring or perverting her natural symmetry. This scene observed by a possibly dead Rebecca Rolfe, who Pocahontas became, becomes very confused. I know these are supposed to be American Indians, but there is so much, not wrong, but disturbed in multiple visions, influenced by the disturbance in Pocahontas's own eyes and in mine, and additional disturbance in the figures, and in the frame of the scene, as if the frame were troubled faintly by vibrations, indistinct other sounds, audible but masked as though the speaker had died and only the tremulations of his voice continue.

"What else should I understand of what looks like a helmet on one warrior's head? A hint of beards vaguely perceived in the wavering line of male chins? The fierce Nordic features of these men on soft, feminine bodies? The effete, long, and slender faces of the women, such straight features? Or of that cherubic curly-haired elder child? What to make of the grotesque element? The woman who appears to gnaw her arm? The bare trees of the hut above the leaved men and women? The middle, beseeching child, ignored by his mother, now seeming as deformed as the seemingly slaughtered monkey, a funny skullcap on his head? Of that really terrifying monkey with his awful downward gesture, tensely reaching through the beech fire to the cherub, while the separate, most masculine warrior watches? The absence of the white men whose ships are in the harbor, transporters noticed only by the tobacco stem bearer, what of that arrival or departure?"

Clark said, "Once more I will remember it, one more time, since you come here to me, in my exile, so openly, with so much eagerness in your faces, you William my brother and you Meriwether and you others.

"You know all that I spoke yesterday and the days before. In March of that same year, 1779, I had as yet sent no message to the tribes, wishing to wait to see what effect our victory would have on them. The Piankeshaws, being of the tribe of Tobacco's Son, of whom you've asked me, were always familiar with us. Part of the behavior of this grandee of the Piankeshaws, as he viewed himself, was diverting enough. He had conceived such an inviolable attachment for Captain Helm, who as I have said had already been taken by the British, that on finding that the captain was a prisoner and not being as yet able to release him, he declared himself a prisoner also. This was all before I came. He joined his brother, as he called Captain Helm, and continually kept with him, condoling their condition as prisoners in great distress, at the same time wanting nothing that was in the power of the garrison to furnish since Governor Long wished to be allied with him.

"As I have just said, the governor, knowing the influence of Tobacco's Son, was extremely jealous of his behavior, and took every pain to gain him by presents; but when anything was presented to this remarkable Indian, his reply would be that it would serve both him and his brother to live on. He would not enter into council with the governor, saying that he was a prisoner and had nothing to say, but was in hopes that when the grass grew again, his brother, the big knife, meaning me, would release him, and when he was a free man, he could talk. Being presented with an elegant sword, he drew it, and, bending the point on the floor, very seriously said it would serve him and his brother to amuse themselves sticking frogs in the pond while in their rather free captivity. In short, nothing could be done with him, and the moment he heard of our arrival, he paraded all the warriors he had in his village and was ready to fall in and attack the fort, but for reasons formerly mentioned was desired to desist.

"As I had Detroit now in my eye, it was my business to make straight and clear a road for myself to walk, without thinking much of anyone's interest or anything else but that of opening the road in earnest —by flattery, deception, or any other means that occurred. With Tobacco's Son at my side and also my interpreter, Drake, who was highly respected among the Piankeshaws and others between St. Vincents and the Lakes as a magician, I told the chiefs who had come to study what I would order in this country, that I was glad to see them, and was happy to learn that most of the nations on the Wabash and Maumee had so far abstained from any action against us, though I had no treaty with them.

" 'Men and Warriors!' I said to them, 'pay attention to my words. You informed me yesterday that the Great Spirit had brought us together, and that you hoped, as He was good, that it would be for good. I have also the same hope, and expect that each party will strictly adhere to whatever may be agreed upon—whether it be peace or war—and henceforth prove ourselves worthy of the attention of the Great Spirit.

" 'I am a man and a warrior, not a counselor. I carry war in my right hand, and in my left hand peace. I am sent by the council of the big knives, and their friends, to take possession of all the towns possessed by the English in this country, and to remain here watching the motions of the red people; to bloody the paths of those who attempt to stop the course of the river, but to clear the roads from us to those who desire to be in friendship with us, that the women and children may walk in them without meeting anything to strike their feet against.

" 'I am ordered to call upon the great fire for warriors enough to darken the land, and that the red people may then hear no sound but of birds who live on blood. I know there is a mist before your eyes. I will dispel the clouds now, that you may clearly see the cause of the war between the big knife and the English, that you may judge yourselves which party is in the right, and if you are warriors, as you profess to be, prove it by adhering faithfully to the party which you shall believe to be entitled to your friendship, and do not prove yourselves to be old women.

" 'The big knives are very much like the red people. They don't know how to make blankets and powder and clothes. They buy these things from the English, from whom they are sprung. They live by making corn, hunting and trade, as you and your neighbors, the French, do. But, the big knives daily getting more numerous, like the trees in the woods, the land became poor where we were and hunting scarce and, having but little to trade with, the women began to cry at seeing their children naked, and tried to learn how to make clothes for themselves. They soon made blankets for their husbands and children, and the men learned to make guns and powder.

" 'In this way we did not want to buy so much from the English. They then got mad with us, and sent strong garrisons throughout our country, as you see they have done among you on the Lakes, and among the French. They would not let our women spin, nor our men make powder, nor let us trade with anybody else. The English said we should buy everything from them and, since we had got saucy, we should give two bucks for a blanket, which we used to get for one. We should do as they pleased, and they killed some of our people to make the rest fear them.

" 'This is the truth and the real cause of war between the English and us, which did not take place for some time after this treatment. But our women became cold and hungry and continued to cry. Our young men got lost for want of counsel to put them in the right path. The whole land was dark. The old men held down their heads for shame because they could not see the sun, and thus there was mourning for many years over the land.

" 'At last the Great Spirit took pity on us, and kindled a great council fire, that never goes out, at a place called Philadelphia. He then stuck down a post, but put a war tomahawk by it, and went away. The sun immediately broke out; the sky was blue again; and the old men held up their heads and assembled at the fire. They took up the hatchet, sharpened it, and put it into the hands of our young men, ordering them to strike the English as long as they could find one on this side of the great waters. The young men immediately struck the war post and blood was shed.

" 'In this way the war began, and the English were driven from one place to another until they got weak, and then they hired you red people to fight for them.

The Great Spirit got angry at this and caused your old father, the French king, and other great nations, to join the big knives and fight with them against all their enemies.

" 'So the English have become like deer in the woods, and you may see that it is the Great Spirit that has caused your waters to be troubled because you have fought for the people he was mad with. If your women and children should now cry, you must blame yourselves for it, and not the big knives.

" 'You can now judge who is in the right. I have already told you who I am. Here is a bloody belt and a white one. Take which you please. Only behave like men, and don't let your being surrounded by the big knives cause you to take up the one belt with your hands, while your hearts take up the other.

" 'If you take the bloody path, you shall leave the town in safety, and may go and join your friends, the English. We will then try, like warriors, who can put the most stumbling blocks in each other's way, and keep our clothes long-stained with blood.

" 'If, on the other hand, you should take the path of peace, and be received as brothers to the big knives, with their friends, the French, should you then listen to bad birds that may be flying through the land, you will no longer deserve to be counted as men, but as creatures with two tongues, that ought to be destroyed without listening to anything you might say for yourselves.

" 'As I am convinced you never heard the truth before, I do not wish you to answer before you have taken time to counsel. We will, therefore, part this evening, and when the Great Spirit shall bring us together again, let us speak and think like men with but one heart and one tongue.

" 'When you return to your own lands, I will send

with you letters of a speech to all the tribes, to pass my word among those who have not come in to us. To them, I wish you, in my speech, to say this,

" ' "Men and Warriors: it is a long time since the big knives sent belts of peace among you soliciting of you not to listen to the bad talks and deceit of the English, as it would at some future day tend to the destruction of your nation. You would not listen, but joined the English against the big knives and spilt much blood of women and children. The big knives then resolved to show no mercy to any people that hereafter would refuse the belt of peace which should be offered at the same time as one of war.

" ' "You remember last summer a great many people took me by the hand, but a few kept back their hearts. I had sent the belts among the nations to take their choice. The big knives are warriors and look on the English as old women and all those that join the English, and we are ashamed when we fight them because they are no men.

" ' "I again send two belts to all the nations, one for peace and one for war. The one that is for war has your great English father's scalp tied to it, and is made red with his blood. All you that call yourselves his children, make your hatchets sharp and come out and revenge his blood on the big knives. Fight like men that the big knives may not be ashamed when they fight you, that the old women may not tell us that we only fought squaws.

" ' "If any of you is for taking the belt of peace, send the bloody belt back to me that I may know who to take by the hands as brothers, for you may be assured that no peace for the future will be granted to those that do not lay down their arms immediately.

" ' "It's as you will. I don't care whether you are for peace or war, as I glory in war and want enemies to fight us because the English can't fight us any longer and are become like young children begging the big knives for mercy and a little bread to eat.

" ' "This is the last speech or writing you may ever expect from the big knives. The next thing will be the tomahawk. And you may expect in four moons to see your women and children given to the dogs to eat, while those nations that have kept their words with me will flourish and grow like the willow trees upon your waters, upon the river banks, under the care and nourishment of their new father, the big knives." '

"So I spoke, expecting that I should shortly be able to fulfill my threats with a body of troops sufficient to penetrate into any part of their country, and by reducing Detroit bring them to my feet entirely. So I did speak, with Tobacco's Son, and Drake who would soon fade from my life, as visible signs by my side.

"Now it is your turn to speak. Now continue to favor me, my auditors, my brother, and my friend, my welcome visitors, with your valuable lessons. Continue to tell me stories of your journey to the western ocean or, if you will, reprimand me as though I was your son. If suspicious, think not that promotion or conferred honor in my past will now occasion any unnecessary pride in me. Your recent Missouri journey, your considerable exploration, has infused too many valuable precepts in me to be guilty of the like. Nor will I show any indifference to those that ought to be dear to me. It is with pleasure I have obeyed in transmitting to you my tired recollections, now that I come near my death.

"Shall I say any more? You too will leave me, departing from me at last, like Drake in a pair of my old breeches, for something newer yet, toward some mysterious destiny of your choice or chance desire perhaps. Beneath us, the Ohio turns white around its rocks; the falls are in bright sunlight which once were so dark in the setting out. Detroit will never fall to me. The colonies will never supply me with the requisite provisions and men. I have been forced to leave my mission forever half-completed; though I won through for them, the country, these states. I won the land which the arguers signed for in France—Franklin and Adams and Jay—and Detroit fell into the argument, not into my hands forever.

"Once more I put off my silence, and once more I try, in memory, undermanned, to move north, once more the advance party, about seventy men, is killed or made prisoners. Only a small boat makes her escape, all that is saved.

"I linger, on this freely given land, after myself. For a long time now I have been unable, as you know, to shoot the once darkened falls, or fish the stiller places with nodding cane poles. They have built a town now across the river, and I sit lonely in my paralysis, except you or the Indians come. I live after myself on this bluff of land. It is my own land, except the road the red people retained to come in to me, as you have come."

Marie said, "Then my name was

Antelope-child, child doomed to be, like a soft rare doe, the meat of warriors, prophesied to be served up for the pleasure and hunger of the warriors, selected at birth from many closed-eyed children, refused the natural grace of childbearing, unusually designed to be a meal for my father, giving insight through his poison and him to the tribe, to the warriors, giving an immortal life to He-who-ate, like the old doe, my mother, like my rabbit-chasing brothers.

"We seldom bore the pipe of peace among us, for my father said our gods were different from the gods of other peoples. Only the buffalo was *very* kind, who lived on the grass stems.

"I am the lover now of the buffalo-man, beneath his shaggy head upon this river, the More-of-time. I am the lover of what the buffalo became. Once I knew the buffalo upon the grass, so fragile his legs, ruled my land and the hearts of my people, beyond all his strife and ours, so peaceful at last after his wandering. Even now, I believe the buffalo remains a tender god of power, moving precariously beneath the strident hump of our worship, beneath the fiery horns and fierce head, tender power to move our hearts which have so long lain frozen, confined in the earth, fighting.

"My father said all other gods than ours were false, degenerated through a failure of power, delusions of foreign tribes, whose men became women soft among bushes. What was true was the spirit of the dog, the fox, the prairie cock, my own clan's white-tailed antelope, the prairie dog, jackrabbit, rattlesnake, the bear wandering south to us, the perennial buffalo, the vulture, Saygun's wolf, all our animals, certainly the god-like eagle and, at last, mysteriously, the recent holy ass under watch, guarded in Tookinfare.

"Our gods were the gods of power, but our gods could die. Only men could achieve a kind of immortality, never defined, as they became like gods in their natural lives. The gods, even when triumphant, were perishing in us, dying in our lives. How could we be serious about such gods? My father said most of our animals were faded gods, gods as they became known to us, that in some animals no god remained perceptible. Only the buffalo, the eagle, the rattlesnake, the antelope, and the new mysterious ass still held, my father said, much of the true powers of gods. He said the buffalo wouldn't last much longer; that the rattlesnake now kept only the power of his poison, the instrument of the shaman; that the antelope would drop all powers when the shaman, my father, died; and that the eagle brought forth the ass, dying in childbirth, beginning to fade, merely enduring an anticlimax now, a waiting out.

"The gods were mortal, were like men who have innumerable, eventually triumphant enemies leagued against them, only a screen of gods around the people, a ring or circle of protection through which enemies, demons, giants, slaying a god would break sometimes, storming from the mountains, down from the west, eventually destroying the defensive circle in an ultimate rush which now approached us. So my father said.

"He said that when a god fell, then was a time for warriors, as we again believed the end was very near, as we believe in the remembered white froth of a vicious ocean, the advance waters of the crushing rock demons, signaling the route for our ancient enemies, water-signed, for those old devils, giants, forever riding down on us, the terrible creatures also both animal and man, the demons riding themselves, riding their bodies out of the mountains, the horrible parodies of Saygun and his eight-legged horse, riding from the hidden places, out of Where-the-earth-sleeps, when gods and men and the conquerors quarrel.

"They were like all-conquering birds of prey, our gods, living like us, protecting us, claws firmly bedded, clutching the earth as they flew near the sun, dropping the earth like a piece of meat, stooping to catch us up in midfall, before we were broken like an egg, doomed to fail, like stars in strange, distant days always approaching too rapidly, when we might remember Saygun stole the asses for us and think the asses no good gift, but just a taunt of demons, useless as our deaths.

"We called our land Where-the-people-walk, and we called the ringed domain of gods Ass-garden, formerly Cloud-lap. Ringed so, we swept over the plains and prairies, swinging about in our seasons between rivers, renewing ourselves as we could, dying to ourselves, walking in death toward Where-the-earth-sleeps, the last journey the journey of the duels. We swept down seasons, over high plains, beneath the threatening mountains, beside the long-grass country or through it too, between rivers we called Dew-fall and Art-of-war or as far east over prairies as the More-of-time, swept like the wild eagles, who also come from the mountains, turning in springtime southward and westward toward the mountains, the way we once came, where we once came from.

"The stony mountains are the eyebrows of Eemire, who was of the earth shattered, father of Saygun the father killer. There, where the people walked, Saygun hovered. He had become a vulture. He was the father of the living gods, blue-gray, cloud-wrapped, hooded with the highest blue of sky, he who was a great father, who was strange and solemn, the always aloof, even as he sat to feast with his children in the guarded place where the holy, unfathering asses brayed out their useless days; even in that sunlike home, Shyforgun; even with our warriors in the creation lodge, he would eat no food, a stranger among us.

"The food was set before him. He gave the food to his two wolves, they who crouch always at his feet, while two black birds perched upon his shoulders. They were the birds who flew each day through the world and returned. They had the doings of men on their tongues, Memory and Thought of the people.

"Saygun, while others ate, pondered his birds, for he constantly sought more wisdom for the days that fail, when the ring of protection is tarnished, when the sensitive ring shall burst under pressure. He would avert our ruin and the ruin of our gods, remains strange as the asses, he among us, protector of people and asses, for he delivers the buffalo and is father of all, blinded in one eye, wearing a wide-brimmed hat pulled over the other. He wears the blue hat and winds the secret of our old mountain writings. He learns to write the words onto wood and metal, onto stone. He suffers for that knowledge many nights, fighting a demon in a pine tree, the battler among branches, Saygun.

"In the tree we have forgotten, he is wounded with a spear like his own; for he is his own offering, and he pulls aside the leaves to reveal the woman who was the key to the inscriptions, a very wise woman, whose tongue is missing from her mouth, the tongue Saygun mourned for.

"He searches the crevices, encounters giants. He pursues Lockjaw, the shifting one who wears the long-eared hat, Lockjaw who is two ways, for who the ass is the key, the prying lever, the likeness that reveals Lockjaw.

"Lockjaw slinks away in a disagreeable form. He has wounded Saygun, in the high tree. He has desired Saygun's wife, who is a secret in herself, never telling what she knew when she accidentally revealed her tongueless body to her husband.

"Saygun's wife takes up her spinning, of a secret purpose. A doe passes, pausing, soft and noble like the people, containing the scene in her body as if it were her child.

"In days, too young as yet to pass, brown-red and blossoming, before the returning god and the sewing goddess, the doe is still too young to be devoured in the clan of my father, Snakesnorter. Too young myself, I have often sung tales of our places, of Where-the-earth-sleeps, Where-the-people-walk, The-tipi-of-immortals, of Ass-garden I have sung, lying young and childless before the feasting, hidden by parents under bushes, as child and maiden, discovered in shame, as my new, secret body was being spun in me, thinking of the asses, unnatural always those animals, strangers to themselves, the hybrids, like the men-horses from who Saygun learned their private breeding, the asses whose future mystery I was born to learn, which is being revealed to me by the asspriest, Pawkittew, holy asses I fled from to the More-of-time, captured by my red-bottomed lover, who I believe I have not yet understood, the fur trapper, my husband who died; so now I am lover at last of the buffalo and what the buffalo becomes, old guardian of our tribe, and I am a white woman with a white man or only an Indian girl listening to secrets from the chief or asspriest I never knew, the half-breed unrevealed by my father; so I am a contradiction, still lecherous, but I will no longer call myself one of the spoken people, as we have called ourselves, people of the buffalo's tongue, who have the same word for animal and story.

"I am conqueror now of the old god—on his fragile legs—the shaggy old head with its piercing down-turned horns, the funny beard like moss, his hump from mountains, who chews to death the fresh pine sprigs that spring throws down from the mountains, his grass-stained tongue. I am his conqueror, he my unwitting woman. Who knows what will come of us, hauling such gold to the people's rendezvous, to the Art-of-war? I am his white woman; he is my shaggy, dark man.

"My marriage ceremony, rite of the maiden, will

never be accomplished, now it's so long postponed,
after the bushes where I lay hidden, Antelope-child,
Deer-maiden, now astounded lover of the buffalo."

Berrigan said, "I have

dreamed tonight, and this morning I have killed
Smith and Thomson, and the Frenchman, Jacques Le-
Guey. We had drunk of the chokecherry wine. The
small buds of new berries will witness my acts, so will
the fire I built for Sawpootway, and the half-breed and
his mule will also witness me. For I had help: first the
subtle girl on the deerskin, then the silent, unfamiliar
Indian, his gray mule trampling the clearing, the red
man diving among my enemies.

"This night I have danced, incomprehensible
dances that transform me, shifting an emphasis, turning a coin or die, so something I don't understand
gives myself away too much for me. I think it might
be too much for me, the new more emphatic face of
coin or die.

"This morning I have remembered Corn Island,
where no maize grew and men were the gathered
grain that Indians invented; the first appearance of the
boy in my eyes, I have remembered; myself, when my
body, out of place on the island, felt too great for me,
too huge and elephantine to control with the human
mind, the tusks shooting like lightning, long ivory
buds, and teeth long and pointed to my solitude, before I was altered in the gathering of the grains, for
the cause of liberty.

"Then I enjoyed the water once more, a changed
man, over the death-in-living, over the transition I
was forced to undertake, and I floated like an iceberg
or the great white bear, white as the coldest god, in

the waters I once spewed and, relapsing into myself, would spew again, so I floated while the river, rushing by beyond the island, ruffled the water where the boy had landed, when my teeth had lost their sharp edge and become like clubs on my tongue.

"Then, standing by the bushes, full with July berries, by the hollow elm trunk, staining my beard with the sweetest, fiercest honey, I grew less lonely, relaxing more, watching the boy, as the lover watches his bathing woman, and the boy mended the guns, stock and metal work, and I returned to some old feelings about myself, as if to a previous existence, while the life of the island, the harvest, passed over me like water, pierced by my almost animal indifference, so my own passage through life became as though through an elephant graveyard, through the awful, prehistoric bones.

"Dutch mattered, so did the fine berries in my stomach, the stolen honey, the elements of wood and metal, if not the very guns, so did the distance between us, as I stood on the inclining hill, emerging from a tiny ravine which the bushes disappeared into: I loved Dutch like that, while I, still-tongued, never announcing myself to him, remained invisible above him, chewing on the waxy comb. The bees hadn't returned to their charred, plundered trunk; I hadn't any need to speak to him then, the secret child, the handy boy—my huge tongue, in the cavernous skull, thundering against the teeth and palate, pronounces now, unstilled, sometimes caressing: Before Marie, Sawpootway, there was Dutch beyond myself, my untouched lover.

"This past night we have all danced in the cabin, forgetting Cantrell, performed our dances in the cabin, surrounded by the black toothlike stumps, and at last

I danced with the girl, Sawpootway, drinking the sharp, berry wine from the brown crock jugs; at last, when Smith and Thomson had not returned, when LeGuey slept on the ragpile, when Dutch slept a sleep like a boy's sleep in his chair at the table, we made our independence dance, revolving, against the motion of clocks, around the table, Dutch, and the candle. In the dance, Sawpootway imitated my own awkward manner, and I returned her copy with one of my own, so we formalized the shuffle, sway, brief meeting of bodies, as she slowed for me to catch her or sped the pace of her departure from me, variation of her style of dancing with my own lack of style, alternating time after time.

"I sang, nothing more really than a series of grunts, rising and falling, which my partner imitated in her own voice, which I returned, as she sped away or I lumbered up close, so my grunting voice became the rhythm, the authority of the dance, dance and music restoring me to myself and projecting myself into the future man I hadn't realized yet: I suffered the dance, its alternating falls and exaltations.

"Sometimes I saw her backside, sometimes her features—dancing forward, dancing backward. Once when she turned from me, and I was gruffly near her, I laid my head on her shoulder. We raised our heads high together, and tore at the air over our shoulders. We growled and left our tooth marks head-high on the doorpost, beside the leather hinges.

"As Dutch moved his head, dreaming, back and forth on the rough table, his arms on its surface, as he dreamed in the candle shadow, we slipped outside, into the tree stumps, into the woods where she led me to the clearing. Gathering dry branches, I felt the dance continue in me as though a dancing bear revolved under my skin, as though in hibernation or in mating a dancing bear turned over inside himself, a kind of dying and dreaming. When I'd built the fire, she danced with me again, and the dancing, our experience of ourselves in motion, changed me from who I had been, and I thought in my life I was fated to discover, in skin within skins, bones layered in my bones, like river sediment, a rich delta land, islands penetrating islands, a gathering of new flesh around a wound, the scar rose, the elephant's folds and ringed tusks, the temporal bark of trees, within me, reflecting my world.

"She stood still in the clearing and I, inspired, danced alone, revolving ideas of myself, through the weaving pattern, shedding the waste life, concentrated on Sawpootway's youth, her own fire-begotten changes, the subtlety of her skin, like unnumbered grains, as she joined me again, the look of old things she surrendered through her eyes, when we moved as partners in the clearing ceremony, the woman turning before me, showing all her sides slowly, both in our shuffling trot, as her back led me around the fire. I staggered after, walking at intervals. All our wine jugs were laid aside. We faced, holding each other's hands. The dance continued with us, changing as we had changed.

"She said, 'I did not know there was such a good shell-shaker living.'

"We stood side by side holding crossed hands. We faced each other, matching palms. We placed our hands upon each other's shoulders. Side by side, we lay arms across shoulders. Facing, I put my fur hat on her head. We stroked each other under the chin. When I placed my hands on her breasts, as we stood side by side, the nipples, rising, tickled my palms.

"She said, 'I am called an old man by my husband, poor and ugly, but I am not this.' She removed my hands with her own and said, 'This is for friendship. We are going to touch each other's privates.'

"She placed my hands upon the cloth above her genitals, laying her own hands on my leather breeches, as I felt the shock in our bodies.

"She told me what to say, standing so still, only her lips moving, and mine tracing in silence her own saying, before I said, aloud, 'I am going to take this woman home with me, as I did not know there was such a good shell-shaker, none like her. I will take her home to my people.' Twice I repeated those translated words.

"Dutch, the boy who taught me to love receded from my important life, like a fading tune, to remain, eventually, like an old hurt in my body, sensitive to the weather, remembered among lightning and dripping clouds, as if he were a fish who escaped from my body, winged from my mouth, wounding the tenderest parts of my mouth, disappearing through the horns that began to bud from my head, out of the white skull, the twin bones arisen. I had forgotten the gold, even Cantrell, as we lay down in the clearing, removing our clothes. Relapsing so, I hugged her hard, as I remembered too much or too little, and we licked each other's mouths, confusing our tongues in motions of healing.

"So I loved her, and, in the jagged lightning, the branches were etched on a pale night sky, like veins of the increasing moon; the stars through the flashy night, apparent stars in the west, devised old stratagems of flight, as I held the subtle girl on the deerskin.

"I knelt between her opened legs, as our campfire, opening like a pale rose, illuminated small speckles dark on the deerskin; so I knew her body's blood was seeping, that she was losing some blood. I enjoyed the eagerness with which she expressed her initial, strongest desire as I entered. So did her nimbleness please me, the limber quality of her whole body. So did her softness like a rotting fig, the overripe fruit. So did the sticky sap my penis felt inside, like the inner layers of a green bud, layers that stick as you peel them, stick more and more, the deeper you go, to your fingers.

"So she was like that green, sappy bud, and so she was like the fruit fallen, which the walker, casually passing the tree, steps on and which he, still casual, pausing, scrapes from his boot with his stick, raising a leg. So I liked each thing in her in itself, but was uncomfortable with the combination, the contradiction I felt in her, as if she wished to be all things at once, the sky and the earth, the fire and the water, the budding thing and the fruit someone should already have plucked and eaten; and so I did not like her so much later, as I was coming, when her smile, so cold and performed, denied my obvious desire and her own. The fig though, I thought, is always a bud, so I sucked at her nipple, the invisible opening in her breast, and burst within her, so my creamy, my saplike water, flooded her bud- or figlike belly, where I had penetrated and found her through the trickling blood which my penis had stopped.

"She turned pale and seemed sunk into herself, the belly collapsed, as I lay beside her, as if she were unfilled or deflated. Her face was drained and tired, as if her darkness had fled into the fire and pale night where sticks in fire and lightning in clouds were thick veins, like snakes, like the twisted brains of an animal once the skull is opened.

"She wished to remove herself, but seemed stuck to my penis, as though our liquids had solidified, so I held myself high to help her escape as she writhed out from under. We both stood, and she held the deerskin up, carefully studying the signs, the speckles of blood, as if they were tea leaves or unfamiliar, telling words.

"She said, 'Now I can be a white woman.' She smiled, her wide mouth trembling in her deepest pleasure; yet she frowned then as if she were uncertain.

"I helped her spread the skin and, when we lay down again, not touching each other, she talked against my silence, carefully, as if each word might help to emphasize or finally reveal her special revelation, spied in the speckled animal leather.

" 'The bears, who dwell in groves, earth curers, world healers, weird figures in childhood stories and visions, awful, protective, dancing bears, bears figured in the hunting song all children learned, the unsecretest song of the bears from the mountains,

> *Now we will surely see the good black things, bears conceived in the rocky land.*
> *The best of all things is to see each other.*
> *I call you out of your lairs, I call you out of your lairs, from the inaccessible places.*
> *I call you out of the chokecherry bushes, where the pool is yellow under the yellow falls, where the pool is gall.*
> *I call you to come from the invisible pool, the good drinking water, the pool hidden from the ordinary hunters.*
> *It seems a yellow and disastrous swamp to them, these commonplace hunters, when they come too near the good water.*
>
> *For the water of the bears is too good for them to drink, in the dangerous place, where the swirl of bees works its sweet ways, and the wild fowl pass, in the full ravine.*

Come to us, bears.
Come to us, bears.
Come to us, bears.
Come to us, bears.
Come to us, bears.
Come to us, bears, come among us, and we shall do you up in the buffalo skin bundles.

Listen to us, our footsteps, our women singing their own song behind us, hear us.
We have your promise, remember.
Remember when we didn't ask your pardon, remember long, how you were angry with the people, forgetting your old human form.
Remember long how you were angry with the people, forgetting.
Now we ask your pardon.
Remember who you were, in the old form, what you did when you left our people, wishing another shape, how you changed among the groves, how you became other than human?
I know you remember how angry you were when the people killed you, without asking your pardon, and the war between us.
Then you came among us, begging peace, afraid to be destroyed by the people?
Do you remember how you gave this song to name you, to ask your pardon?
Do you remember how you pleaded, that you didn't mind that we would kill you, if we'd give you another life, and you gave us an order of song that could change you?
When we kill you, you will not die forever, but will be reborn through us.

Listen, bears, we sing with the women, offering tobacco.
Hear your song.
Hear your song.
Hear your song.

This is the song you gave us.
This is the song you gave us.
This is the song you gave us.
Hear your song.
This is the song you gave us.
Remember when you became the creatures who, killed
and eaten, are able to be reborn. Here is your tobacco,
take it, smoke the tobacco with which we ask your par-
don, smoke the gift.
We have done as you taught us, take the song.
Here is my hand, you bears.

" 'And I remember the story Snakesnorter, my father, chanted to me often, in his dull voice, of the bears when they were powerful,

" ' "In the blue clay bank, by the yellow falls, the dancing grizzly bear spirit lives, in the rocks. From that place they came for me to bestow their blessings on me, to tell me, that should I ever meet with some sudden trouble, they would arrive to aid me. They told me I could offer them as much tobacco as I wanted, that they would always accept and smoke the gift I brought.

" ' "There, by the stilled pool, where the wild falls had dwindled, they gave me some songs, and they gave me, thereby, a way of beholding them, a holy sight.

" ' "The spirits danced, exhibiting their powers in movement. They tore open their wombs, then made themselves holy again and healed themselves. They shot their claws at each other, like little horny knives, out of their soft fur, out of their skins, and they stood there, choking with their blood, then made themselves holy and cured themselves.

" ' "They gave me the songs, and the holy things their claws had become."

" 'I remember, when the first blood flowed from my body, when I was covered by the brush the older women tied upon me, in Maiden-lodge, where I waited for a man to come to steal me, through the food door, wondering who should be my husband if no one came for me, when I was hidden in the bushes, I had a vision of tiny dancing bears, revolving beneath the cottonwood poles. A bear too large for the oval lodge appeared before me, while the small bears danced. He took a bite from my thigh, which didn't hurt me. Carefully molding the scar, he healed me, surrounding my wound with my own squeezed flesh. He made blood flow from a length of skin he hid in my wound. He was too large for the room we had. The bleeding did not last long, so the women unbound me. They removed me from the lodge, and dipped me in The-Art-of-war, in the river.

" 'I returned to the tribe, safely crossing the game paths, and while my father considered my future, while my nameless mother wept, Jacques LeGuey opened the food door to appear in my mind's lodge, wrinkled and shorn. He told me, as I lay in my shame, that he would marry me as though I were a white woman, so I squeezed hard on my heart. Since the bleeding had stopped in my womb and from the length of skin the bear had hidden, my new mind pumped my heart, blowing fire from it, and I willed, intensely, the bursting which didn't come soon enough, and I came to desire LeGuey—later to desire every man—his furry penis like a buttocked tail between his thighs, his blood-shaded bottom, red and purple, so terribly mysterious and desirable to me. Yet I could never understand him as I wished and, when I had squeezed all the blood from my heart, and bled from the womb for him, he refused to touch me, left me ashamed in the bushes, concealed from him in my pains, alone in the wrong order of things, with no way to discover myself to pretending parents or to my false husband.'

"Then I slept deeply, dreaming of approaching summer, then of winter coming, of hibernating bears asleep in my flesh, deep in the caves of me, in my facing walls; of deer, with tiny hoofs, breaking into my skin, as through ice, to drink at my secret pools; of a big land lizard, burning from the inside, flaming outward, becoming palely pink as a prairie rose, odorless, without smoke. The lizard surveyed, from his leaning pink and yellow rock, sleeping bears and thirsty deer. I dreamed of the jutting stony mountains, greater than I'd ever seen. It was like no other dream; it had an authority for me no common dream has, as if it retold my past and indicated my future exactly.

"When I woke, Marie had gone. Daylight had almost come. The fire burned low, yet still cast their shadows, three shadows blurred, two of them like one shadow; so I fought before I even saw the glinting knives, stood on the hillock and fought, the dust flying aside beneath my grinding moccasins, as they came on.

"At first I didn't know who the third man was. Memory has dimmed in places, has lost part of the battle, so I see a diminished suddenness and feel that some time I stood hugging Smith or Thomson to me, while the one of them I didn't hold climbed up my back. The third man had fallen, unwounded, beneath me, and I felt the fang of Smith or Thomson's knife graze my forehead, the other's blade edge part way through my shoulder.

"I felt no pain, only heat, and didn't know till later that I bellowed, as if calling aid, my one low roar the only loud noise of our action. Then the Indian arrived and it was over. I felt Smith or Thomson's back break under my pressure. A weight was lifted from my back to be replaced by another weight on my shoulders, like the heaviness of the wound I'd received.

"I recognized the Frenchman on the ground, where I'd just flung him. I was squeezing the second of the other men as LeGuey began to rise again. I released the dying Smith or Thomson and kicked out at the darkness. I found I'd stamped the small body of Le-Guey into the ground. I saw the half-breed hover over the faces of the fallen, threatening to demolish their flesh as they tried to rise again.

"All fell back in death—Smith and Thomson flung far aside—as I collapsed upon the Frenchman, trying to understand my anger for this one man. The Indian pulled me off and, leaning, cut small nicks in the Frenchman's features, and in Smith's and Thomson's, drawing no blood or the least possible blood invisible in darkness, small signs of his own preoccupation. I wandered off, nauseous, wiping my own blood where it had flowed over my face, throwing my body forward, gradually coming erect as I walked the fight off.

"I stumbled upon Marie and the boy, young Dutch, and said, 'I believe it was the gold. I believe it could not have been anything else, except for the Frenchman.' I looked at Marie. She looked away from me.

"Dutch said, 'What is it? What is for the gold?'

" 'I've killed Smith and Thomson, also the French-man.'

"I could go on, now I had felt the knife turning around my shoulder bone, cleanly, now Marie would come back to me and I would love her, now that she would clean the small wound on my forehead and the wound of my upper back. Now I wouldn't even need rest, seeing how she saw me as she looked at me again, as she moved toward me. Now we would have the gold for what it was worth to us, and we would await the reappearance of Cantrell without anxiety. Now I was aware of the Indian and his mule behind my shoulder, when I turned, how his eyes were only for Dutch, the German boy who stood open-mouthed, hands fiddling with his breeches as if he were not sure they were closed properly. He rolled his eyes from Marie to me, seeing the half-breed Indian and the mule then. I saw Dutch's fear as he saw them.

"When I collapsed, the half-breed and Dutch began to lift me, but I sat up, removing my shirt, exposing the rosy knife wound in my shoulder. I was not so changed yet: I let Marie apply the water, her fingers in the torn lips of flesh; I let her fetch the spider's web I asked for, which stopped my blood inside the shoulder; I let her tear her dress in long strips of white bandages; I let her apply the strips fresh from the water, washing my forehead, tying them on my back where the pain grew like a hump under the skin; I let her doctor me as she wished—but I was, in the end, my own cure of myself: rising to collect the shovels, to let Dutch help me bury my dead; while Marie tried to love me before I was ready, transformed, to love her fully.

"So I would not let her touch me if I could help it, at the graves. I had not returned to consciousness yet, though the hump of pain began to grow dull on my shoulders. I dug the grave for Smith and Thomson, while Dutch made the one for her husband, a mystery to me I didn't want to touch, while Marie tried my patience with her touch. The Indian interpreter and his mule watched, from their distance, mostly Dutch.

"I could not bear to have her touch me yet, till part was buried with Smith and Thomson, now I began to understand them, within the mystery of my anger at the little trapper, who was so mangled as if in lust."

Drake said, "I see the men

through the wide fire, see more clearly first Clark standing alone to my left, observing his instruments, the Jeffersonian forces, instruments of his powerful will for Detroit, his drive he hopes will cleanse the nation of the British influence. All his life he will turn toward France as the place through which his English consciousness discovers America, toward the first dark place he can think of. It will ruin him politically, when he champions the minister Genet; yet he will die with Jefferson in the presidency and his own hopes for the country renewed. I begin to see Clark already wrong, in the willful pursuit.

"I see two figures lumped under the trees to my right, the larger obscuring the smaller, neither of who I can yet recognize as separate from the other men, until the two do separate for a moment: Berrigan and Blau.

"I see also the man called Cantrell standing in the circle of men, speaking to them in a high voice. He confuses me. I have considered him eligible to be He-for-whom-we-seek-life only in the desperate moments that come as the time draws nearer, on this February twelfth.

"I have seen the buffalo again today, a small herd almost submerged in the burning water. Today I have watched the fish burning on sticks at the flames, watched the games Clark improvised for his men, seen the men settling into a natural dullness as Clark spoke of Indians and the buffalo, while they smiled at him.

"Now I continue the story of my ancestors to the invisible men—faces cleansed, in the flames, of their features—the longest story I've yet told them, as incomprehensible as the picture to them. They stare from the cleansed faces when the fire illuminates them at instants. They would smile at me from those faces, the features clearer, if I spoke again our lesser tribal stories, amusing them as they condescend to me; but I am still thinking of the picture of the white man's arrival or departure, and I am troubled by other voices of wills imposed on mine.

"What should I understand of the sense of disturbing voices: Rebecca Rolfe's and perhaps someone else's, hesitant as if after death, as if reluctant to reveal their persons—a sense of one who speaks now only because he cannot bear the bitterness, the flushed rose to bitter yellow transformations, in my half-breed voice, in my distorted will, cannot stand what I might have done to the story had I been let alone; and a sense of another, a willful woman of insistent sound, occasionally relaxing, hinting at a version other than her historical story of the ruff, the shore death at departure, the English child. My vision, disgusted, moves on into activity.

"Two white hunters enter a valley. They carry a deer on poles between them. I know I see her now, and the white men see her. She is already, as a young girl, fully a woman. She reclines on the soft, damp turf, knees raised, touching the earth with her feet and buttocks, with the hands with which she supports herself.

"She lies naked, of course, below now as well as above the waist. She tells the two hunters, who are a white man and an Indian, to leave her for now, to return when a year has passed. Her eyes are dark, but bright like fire close to what it burns. Her vision contaminates the valley as with flames, opening and spreading.

"They see her around the fort, the powhatan's daughter, the princess, all that waiting year. She no longer seems the same to them. They see her playing with the young boys, in the market, at a game of wheelbarrow. The boys fall upon their hands, raise their heels. Their tongues loll out of the boyish mouths, drag along the ground as Pocahontas wheels them.

"They wheel Pocahontas, as her grass skirt falls open to reveal her buttocks and smooth hairless cunt. She's tumbled, turned, spun through the market.

"The hunters, two white companions, wish they were the boys. They are sad as they understand she has not lived much more than a decade of their lives. The one who has just been an Indian fishes with his cane pole near the woods. Pocahontas appears to bathe with the young women of her tribe. She caresses the fisherman and cries repeatedly, while her girls and women laugh, 'Do you love me? Do you love me?'

"At the end of the year, the white man and the Indian return to the valley. She isn't there. In her place, crops grow: beans where her right hand and foot had touched the earth, corn where her left two had touched, and tobacco where her twinned buttocks once rested. They hear her voice, echoing throughout the hills, tumbled through the valley, 'Do you love me? Do you love me?' Her speech demands more than ever before, her insistent, querulous voice.

"The two hunters fall asleep to her spoken rhythms, two white men lulled by her Indian tongue as it speaks their own language, their own accents falling as if to mock them. They were horizontal figures, elongated dark humps of the landscape, appearing, as darkness grew fuller, to be Indians.

"What has flowed from the picture flows on, as if attempting to define itself more clearly in the receding landscapes, figuring America, the current beneath a more social or external fabric above waters, beneath the mission of Clark and his troopers, as I watch their anonymity perverted by the rosy alterations of the campsite.

"Pocahontas continues: the famous scene. Captain John Smith arches his back against a stone. Her ferocious father, imperious, raises his tomahawk, peace pipe inverted, as if he were his daughter's husband or lover. The dusky maid, lighter now than the rest of her tribe, cradles the captain's head, blue eyes and red hair, in her now muscular arms. It is a scene of protection, of the embrace, of the war instrument.

"I see her whitening face, for which John Smith will reject her. She will no longer be his lover. What remains will be for John Rolfe, her new father, the husband, my ancester. And, for a moment, it is Rolfe I see, who weds her against my expectation, who adopts her other than the powhatan adopts John Smith.

"Smith remains somehow a white man, perhaps a new kind of white man, moving through forests in search of dark, temporary lovers, while Rebecca Rolfe's once red skin is almost forgotten in the transition over the ocean, skin left lying in fragments in natural forest clearings for serpents to wonder at. The torn member of their species the animals and Indians must think her, seeing the old skin Pocahontas has shed among her nation, in the landscape she has disappeared from almost entirely, only her relics among woods, vaguely, brightly patterned, possible reminders of a goddess who has fled her dominion, abdicated the fluted throne of serpents, seeking an ideal life among white women like the Queen, new women savage to her in her new life. At least once, those women must originally have appeared to her, surely, as the savages they were, so I hope, the white witches, icy bitches of the curs disclosed in my vision now, at the scorched water, on this flooding red ground.

"In the present vision, land reemerges through the waters, fire in the air.

"I see Metacomet, the fierce Miami. He haunts the whited woman like a dark ghost, aided by his medicineman Grimesco. He pursues her love, rivaling Smith. He is the terrible, wholly Indian, Metacomet, Smith's opposite. He asks the white captain why the English, professing such great love for England, should want to cross wide seas to deprive the poor Indian of rude and savage forests only an Indian could love. At the peace festival, the wedding of races, Metacomet, resistant, eternal enemy of whites, sworn, follows a westward-bending star, with dark eyes among the turkeys, the pumpkins. Metacomet flies, divided by the girl, commits his suicide on the banquet table, asserts his nativity forever beyond the grasp of invaders, flees toward unmolested liberty, after the star. The field is clear now for John Rolfe. Metacomet's orating voice no longer fills the scene, this clearing made by Rolfe's embrace with Pocahontas.

"Smith, the powhatan's new son, the best man watches. He is the rescued male forever in his dreams. He lived once through Pocahontas, lady-rescuer, his Ariadne, her sex and race his thread and needle; and he remembers so much that has already happened, now merely indicated in the moving picture frame.

"In the first danger, long ago, he gave his compass to Powhatan, as an instrument of magic, the west-discoverer's, Indian-finder's, new coast-mapper's, quadrant bow, and it almost worked to his delivery, when he spoke, 'I have demonstrated by the globelike jewel, the roundness of the earth and skies, the sphere of the sun, moon, and stars, and how the sun did chase the night round about the world continually; the greatness of the land and sea, the diversity of nations, varieties of complexions, and how we are to you antipodes.' The Indians stood amazed with admiration.

"John Smith knew what he was talking about, keeping antipodal in his mapping search for temporary alliances and a new life for white men; he was the great romancer, couldn't tell a story straight ever. For three successive days, he suffered the symbolic rites of Indians dressed as devils, trying to frighten him. He saw the Indians at Meronocomo wonder at him, as if he were a sea monster. He sat before a fire, on a seat like a bedstead, covered in a great robe of raccoon skins, tails dangling all over his body. He sat there with young wenches, potential rescuers, at each hand. Two rows of men stood on each side of the captive, as many women behind the double rows. All their heads and shoulders were painted red, as if their natural skins weren't colored enough. Many of their heads were buried under white bird down and they wore strings of white beads around their necks as if prophesying a future submergence of the red man in the white tide from the ocean.

"The Queen of Appamatuck, appointed, brought water from the shore, and Smith washed his hands and dried them on the feathers she also brought him. They feasted him, consulted, concluded, then brought two great stones. They dragged him, laid his head on the stones, ready with clubs to beat out his brains. He lay prone on the rocks. There was an archness in his spine. The club was raised that didn't fall. Pocahontas sheltered her own head in his arms and his head in hers.

"John had already almost forgotten her. He rose as the powhatan's new son. She was content with English toys and trifles. The emperor received hatchets, bells, beads, copper, though he'd been promised two great cannons and a grindstone. But the discharge of the cannon frightened his people, and the grindstone proved too heavy to transfer. Like Metacomet, he was never content.

"Soon we see the first American wedding, of the Rolfes, celebrated in feasting, with the adoption of John Smith. Pocahontas becomes Smith's sister who their father gives away from them in the marriage to Rolfe. John Smith loses interest in her, sees her direction, a lost sister impossible to avenge.

"Pocahontas is transported, appears as Rebecca Rolfe in the court of King James, stands before the queen, a slightly dark English lady now, whose manners and appearance draw approving comment from court ladies over catty asides, and the courtiers dance with the dusky lost princess, then stand about corners snickering, like boys in a schoolyard wanting to scratch their balls.

"Rolfe wills Pocahontas to be portrayed as an exaggeration of this woman in the court, his slightly exotic English wife, Christian Rebecca Rolfe. He insists on the stiff European clothes which will descend, immortalized, through generations not their own, in the only picture history will possess of her, the white lady.

"When he receives this portrait from the artist, my ancestor, John Rolfe, suffers a revulsion at her oiled reflection, the picture so perfectly what he proposed. He suffers the death that precedes transformation. She seems to him now the white termagant wife, some horrible, too familiar, beautiful bird who preys on her male young. He hides their son, Thomas, in Heidelberg, and arranges for a voyage back to America, to return her. He only just arranges, and falls, as they wait for the ship to sail, into a deep sleep which lasts twenty years. Then, when she is dead, he wakes as his own son. The woman is dead, never sailing back to America. The new Rolfe is free. He returns to America in search of the original Pocahontas, recovering the young man his father had been, gone fishing.

"When he's gone, Rebecca Rolfe, of the portrait, rises purely from Pocahontas's ashes, like a white swan, beautiful, transcending her past. She moves toward America."

Berrigan said, "I did find
the gold, in the low draw, recognizing the scene where I'd been with the others. I dismounted to play the fool. I pulled my hat down over my ears, performed an awkward silly jig trot up and down the bank, tumbled down, falling with my face in a thin trickle of water, and I rose with a smile. The sun burned its own way down toward the Mississippi. When I looked at the others, moving darkly behind the tree, the sun, brighter and hotter, stunned me. I felt suddenly cold as the breeze touched my sweating body, and slightly dizzy, while my wounds burned and the scene took on for me the character of dream, faded and recovered near waking.

"I dreamed the others behind the tree, others I could clearly see as dark spots, in the surface of the western sun, falling forward through the light. Dutch brought the wagon up, while the other two, the Indians, Marie and Drake, accompanied him. They were all still laughing at me.

"The sun stung the membranes of my eyes, made my eyes weepy, and I conceived those figures, my dark pupils open in the cool shadow of the others. When I dreamed the others, I felt the sun breaking through the surface into my sockets and veins, into the curious refinement of my brain, spreading down toward my toes, as I felt still dizzy, as what I took to be new skin developed inside me, the dun-rose flush of the new, interior membrane, as the sun's male organ sought me out in the ravine.

"I saw Marie clearer, with renewed desire, as Antelope-child, the child she once was, and the sun surfaced in me as I felt still and foolish. Dutch lifted the gold bars from the black hole in the wet earth. Drake covered the bars with furs that had belonged to the trapper and reburied them in the wagon. Sun, Marie, and the gold blazed through me, to the limitation of my skin, as the long bars passed, raised by Dutch from the black hole through the fingers of Marie, who handled them unnecessarily. Drake placed them in the furred wagon. I sank in the bright dream, the dark hump and horns of my fur cap hot on my head, as I touched the furs, and felt the fire inside me meet the hidden burnished fire of the gold, the combination rushing into the landscape that opened before me to reveal my companions calling me away.

"I felt myself pregnant with a vision, myself the medium of some future, of some visionary child I could only identify with the landscape of figures, a child the fire sought out, to be revealed in the continuous alternations of the low river hills, in the transformations of the earth as intimate spring mimicked the beginnings of my summer. I knew intimations of a transforming landscape as yet concealed far beyond the river.

"When we'd crossed that water, arcing, to Ste. Genevieve, and passed on up the river to Pain Camp or St. Louis, arriving at the confluence of the Missouri and Mississippi—near a pool of water reflecting the campfire, I loved her as if in previous dream, recurred or continued after an insignificant lull, loved in her that Antelope-child, sought out the puckered mouth, grazed down her landscape upon the sharp figlike tips of her breasts, which burst in my mouth, peered by firelight beneath her dense fur into the folds of her, into the pink variety of her lips, as if into the inside of the petaled fig, into the deepest rare violet. Her springs opened warm with her own blood to my fingers, my tongue deep in the penetrated fruit, while the clear saplike juice was sticky in my beard; and, when Antelope-child removed my own new-bought layers of clothing—buffalo hat, bearskin coat, the blue-white veined vest, and tusk-yellow pants—she received my penis, as we stared at each other before we began to move, stared in a kind of fear while we experienced a confluence of fires, of our surfacing blood, external in me, buried in Antelope-child, knowing each other alike in our difference.

"My skin flushed as dark as hers and existed against her skin as, with my mammoth bones, I flattened her out more than ever beneath me, as we moved until I filled her with the yellow-ivory of our conquest, the golden marrow of my white bones. Her body grew paler, I saw, than mine, yet fiery, a near landscape of the flesh flying away, whose fires I believed I could discover again and again, the burnished gold risen in us, in that morning, in the crotch of Mississippi and Missouri, in that entry to the West.

"She rose decidedly from my body, the gold I'd discovered, the gold that I'd seen was hers, rising with her, in her departing body, sparkling up toward the morning blue of the sky, against which she seemed to blend, blue and white, only her hair still dark as the blood as she rose, red-tinted falls descending long and separately, as if I had, after all, broken through the last membrane into her flood, so that it fell then from her ascending head.

"She stood erect and her hair flowed smoothly then over her shoulders as if her body, like a rock, shed the burning waters. My steam expended, I dressed myself, and felt that she had taken me as the sun had, as a man takes a woman, too far from myself, ravished me, and I saw, through the trees we rose under, the half-breed, Drake, opposite the rising sun, walking with Dutch in the broad clearing of the prairie.

"We lovers moved to join them where they walked, and we departed up the Missouri, into the western landscape, hauling gold. Drake said it was the direct route to Santa Fe.

"In the May crossing, of new land along the first westward extension of the Missouri, through rolling hills across finger valleys ascending from mountains, from the Mississippi, over the deeply carved prairies, while the basic land rose continually, imperceptively, and the hills rose and fell, as we approached the Kansas, and trees were gradually disappearing, the landscape beginning to flatten out beneath the more naked grass, I moved after the Indian, as the wagon became more and more of a burden, beneath the farthest downflung fingers of the glacier line, I began to lose the feeling of dampness always deep in the flesh, liquid which froze like marrow in the bones by morning —the body waking stiff and hard, the skin pores tightly sealed like ice-blue morning glories which open to the westward intention of the sun toward noon, then drooping as the sun descends, exaggerating the flesh's natural progress toward its high then oblivious times: each day our steps were freer, and only the wagon held us back.

"I moved against the Missouri as the sweating river, deeply channeled, writhed like a restless serpent, fevered, into new courses, throwing off its skins several times a shedding season, thrusting its westward expansion back from its eastern mouth, and driving the southbent Mississippi against her eastern bank, as the long tail heaved among the courses, convulsing itself. The river, Missouri, vomited, in a thick dark current: decaying vegetation—eight-foot grass, fifteen-foot weed, wild grape, currant, plum, cherry, papaw, persimmon, walnut, pecan, hickory nut, the fallen acorn; whole forests—gigantic sycamore, walnut, cottonwood, linden trees, willow, poplar; islands, sand bars, mud oats; his abundant animals—deer, bear, elk, turkey, and, even, in the spring flood water, the floating carcasses of buffalo in thousands, victims of thawing ice who, heedlessly, had tried to cross the upper icy reaches, their dark bodies cresting the flood; and the rush of fish borne under—teeming trout, bass, perch, and pike; while birds, in the frequent seasonal migrations—pigeon, goose, duck, crane, swan, pelican, gull—passed darkly, limitless, beneath the increasing sun, while wheeling clouds of buzzards attended the river's manifestation of violent and abundant death.

"While Dutch wrote in the small red notebook, leaning toward the fire, while Marie messed her fingers in the thick, dark hair at my neck, while Drake looked at me sideways, I said, 'If we could just avoid the mountains, that's all. At least the mountains.'

"Drake stared at me dully and said, 'No.'

"I was only being difficult, just resistant, for causes I didn't understand, to the half-breed's stated purpose, and I knew I was being difficult, so I said, 'All right, but I'd rather go into the mountains farther south, off of the plains.' We had argued it all before, on the way from Pain Camp, almost four hundred miles winding along the Missouri to this place south of the confluence with the Kansas.

"All the way I had argued we should turn south at this point, but I couldn't win an argument. The half-breed was the only one that knew the full route. I said, 'I don't see why we should go to Marie's tribe. I don't see it.'

"Marie said, 'Why do you care?'

"I didn't know why I cared. Perhaps I was jealous. She and Drake were together often, talking quietly when I couldn't hear.

"I said to Drake in anger, 'Tell me. What are you? You aren't Piankeshaw really, I know that. Are you a Lake Indian at all?'

"Drake's head was turned away. When he spoke, his voice seemed clumsy from hesitation. He said, 'No, I was adopted by the Piankeshaw.' I had stood and was about to say something else when he added, 'I am from one of the tribes west of here, from what white men now call the great desert, on their maps. From near the mountains.'

"When we'd eaten, I watched Marie and Drake from a distance, heard them speaking, sometimes overheard the alien tongue, foreign to me but a tongue common to both of them. They had often walked so, in similar distances. In such appearances, I conceived that Marie made sexual advances to Drake, but that he wouldn't acquiesce to her, only speaking to her for a long time, while her head sank lower until it seemed to hang on her breasts. So I came to trust the half-breed more than I would have otherwise, listening to the distant sound of the male Indian voice, which in its soft resonance seemed consolingly familiar, as sparks from the campfire wound up toward the treetops, and I watched Dutch write in near total darkness.

"We all sat by the fire then, under a full moon, passing the tomahawk pipe which Drake carried with him, puffing our stingy allowance of daily tobacco, and Dutch read the entry for the day, as he had before, squinting close to the writing, hurting his eyes and burning his face at the fire, so we could confirm the account he'd obtained from his own observations and ours.

" '*June 28th.* At one mile on the 26th we passed a muddy little stream at the end of a small island, which was about 30 yards wide at its mouth and flooded, where it entered the Missouri. The Missouri current, very dark, was confined in a narrow bed between the high rock wall and the counter-currents whirling on one side. There the river bent before diverging slightly.

" 'We saw a small island and a sand bar. We shot at a deer. As usual, we went very slowly and Orcus wished to take to the prairie, but the rest of us disagreed. I preferred, for my part, the nearness of the river in this strange country instead of the presence of so much land, increasing so that I found it frightening.

" 'After only 9¾ miles we camped at the mouth of the Kanzas River. Here we have remained two days, during which Orcus and I, Marie accompanying, have made some observations.

" 'On all sides the country is fine, but the waters of

the Kanzas have a very disagreeable taste, even more peculiar than the loam-tasting Missouri.

" 'The Kanza tribe resides on its banks. They have been reduced and banished by the Saulks and Ayauways, who, being better supplied with arms, have an advantage, although the Kanzas are not less fierce or warlike than themselves.

" 'Yesterday at one o'clock we met two rafts loaded, the one with furs, the other with the tallow of buffalow. They were white men returning from the north of the Missouri, on their way to Pain Camp. We questioned one of them, a Mr. Durion, about the plains. He has lived with the northern nations more than 20 years, and is high in their confidence.

" 'He told of an encounter with the Kanzas at the meeting of the river of that name and Missouri rivers, where we are camped. Later in the day we found here the body of a young Kanza woman, hung by the neck from a maple, where the vultures were at her. Orcus cut her down, and he and I buried her where she fell.

" 'We met a raft made of two canoes joined together, in which two French traders were descending from 80 leagues up the Kanzas, where they had wintered and caught great quantities of beaver, but had lost much of their game by fires from the prairie.

" 'These two groups made the first white men we have seen since La Charette, and I suspect the last for a long time, as there will be none in the plains.

" 'They told us that the Kanza nation is now hunting buffalow in the plains, having passed the last winter on this river, which the two Frenchmen call the Kah, a kind of nickname.

" 'Two mile further we reached the mouth of Little Manitou creek, which takes its name from a strange figure resembling the bust of a man with the horns of a stag, painted on a projecting rock, which may represent some spirit or deity, though Drake will not say, since if it is a god they no longer believe in it. The same he said of an eagle painted more clearly on the top of the projection, so you can't see it unless you climb up, which Orcus and I did, and Marie, as Drake laughed at us. Orcus and I have seen similar signs in the past, during our westward journey from Corn Island, especially the rock paintings near Kaskasky.

" 'Today we saw also the tracks of some Indians, and toward evening, after we had buried the poor Kanza girl, buffalow or bison ranging almost as far as eye can see, at least very far. The sun was very red in our eyes, illumining their dark humps, their heavy heads with drowsy eyes. We rode among them, ignored, as far as the cows with young calves huddled in the center of the herd.

" 'We retreated to build our campfire, on these prairies more uncovered, with scattered trees and grapes and other plant life, than those of the Illinois. While night comes we watch the descending sun which burns across the great herd, and I was melancholy, saddened, thinking of the past too much, till Orcus broke my mood, stomping on his buffalow hat he bought in Pain Camp, and crying out to us that he did not need it any more, that now there were here real buffalow. So big in the firelight he was, and I thought he might throw off all his clothes, amusing us, and we were all glad then we had seen the great herd of buffalow, and I was no longer sad, seeing the departing sun behind Berrigan, Orcus Berrigan, awesome as the prairie fires the two Frenchmen had told us of, these buffalow spreading out into the blackness of night, dispersed as if into our dreams.

" 'Drake has said we will dream of ourselves this night, riding differently in the morning. Later we heard some Indians, Drake said they were, hallowing from far off, making animal calls.'

"Listening to Dutch's voice, which sounded even farther away than the two Indians had walked before, I held Marie and felt a regret regarding the young man, Dutch, regretting our separation. I saw the clearness of Dutch in the firelight, heard the distance in his reader's voice, hearing only intimations, in the read-out writing, of the loved one's speaking voice. I felt the loss of an essential past, of an irretrievable first love.

"Marie began to whisper confused Indian and French images of love into my ear, and I felt her breasts heavy against my ribs and heart; but I loved her and saw images, visions she evoked, whispering our future life together in Santa Fe, where I didn't believe either of us would ever go, visions intended to discover a Latin living with our gold.

"We would instead, I thought, be captured in plains, wandering from mountain sources down widening rivers, dried beneath the sun like pegged-out skins of animals, buried in winter beneath the dominating white blizzards of a great plateau, waiting for future white men to uncover us.

"Before we slept, Drake drew me aside and told me, as though it explained all, that he and Marie were of the same tribe, and he said, 'I am also eager to see our people again, you see.' "

Drake said, "I rose—and my mule rose pulling a turn in the traces—before the eyes of the others, walking before Berrigan and Sawpootway, who talked of their future, on the high seat; before Blau, who rode behind Berrigan's horse and Sawpoot-

way's; before the horses tied to the wagon of gold. We rose, winding near the creek, through the blue flint hills, hills bare but for the covering grass, which grew gradually shorter, the short mixed with the tall, as we moved west of the Missouri and Kansas.

"In the hills of flint, I rejoiced, moving for miles through a buffalo herd. It was the treeless land we'd come to, where only a few struggling trees grew isolated on the creek banks or along the lusher Arkansas, The-art-of-war.

"We avoided the lick of a fire that rolled northeast unchecked, over the smoothed mounds, over the short buffalo grass above the eternal matted roots. The land to the southwest, all the way to the horizon, became a single layer of burned grass blades, like a skin over the flint, the advancing line of flame composed of unnumbered tongues we heard whispering overland, easily leaping the sparse creeks, the tiny rivers. I understood the distance and the speed of the fire, and led us swiftly to safety; and the low fire swept on, darkening the land, becoming a barrier of tongues behind us, the blackened hills a backward boundary of our journey, introducing my land.

"Mine was a land where trees had disappeared into animals and men, the once-rooted woods become mobile and fleshy, quickening in the landscape which, visible beyond the hills now, appeared as flat, featureless, as the spread palm of my hand. The trees had become the herds of buffalo and the herds, now almost as great, of our wild plains' horses.

"It was a land where I'd been before, the oceanic bank rising gently toward the blue and white, invisible stone of mountains, the almost imperceptible hills stretching west in their low waves, which could conceal, sometimes, lush, sudden surprises between the crests: a herd—of buffalo, pronghorned antelope, horses—a fire, a tribe, or even a river.

"Here Blau and Berrigan faced a wind more fiercely continuous than they'd ever known, from the southwest now, a terrible current which knew no obstructions.

"It was, after all, my land and Marie's we entered from the blue humps of the hard hills; and my land lay like a dun woman alternately emerging and receding, the woman in the landscape, the figure on fire, under the wind's fierce hot caress in the dominating sun, the figure which I discovered again in the dun and green June earth I would never depart from, relearning eventually both the sun and whitest blizzard, the land's summer assumption, acceptance of sky, and the cold descent of a polar winter, reception of harsh, ceremonious death and burial, death and life in the alterations of a figure, as in a woman's body, her figure so spare that I must fill it, her dark and white alteration, with my mind, creating a plenum of the imagination, perhaps emphasizing the surprises—the gigantic herds, the rivers, the fires, the tribes, the entry of white and red renegades—in the creation of an extensive alter life, an unending vision, dun-blooded or blizzardly white. When Blau and Berrigan entered with Sawpootway and me, it was summer remaining present and undefined in our lives, discovered, despite my landscape-figuring woman, only in the sense that we had arrived in the place."

Drake said, "This night, February twentieth, I speak only to Berrigan and Blau, tell the continuing story only to the two; for the other men

have their own bloody inventions of the conquest of Vincennes and Detroit, their pathetic and childish visions of their own importance, which they no longer conceal even from themselves. I have heard them speak openly of killing all Indians, while Clark smiled down on them. I will stand beside Clark once more, in one more moment of patience or curiosity, as he speaks to assembled chiefs and warriors; but now I sit speaking mainly to Berrigan, observing the huge man's casual motions, in this darkness where a hump of land protrudes from darker waters, intruding into darker air, a piece of land distant from the low campfire and the voice of Cantrell urging the violent talk on, while I say that:

"Thomas Rolfe, grandson of John Rolfe, enters the wilderness as if he meant to throw his life away. He is preserved miraculously among the natives. One male Indian he discovers, and cries to him, 'I never asked thee leave to let me love thee. I have a right. I love thee not as something private and personal, which is *your own,* but as something universal and worthy of love, *which I have found.* You are purely good; you are infinitely good. I can trust you forever. I did not think that humanity was so rich. Give me just an opportunity to live. Consent only to be what you are. I alone will never stand in your way. I would like to be as intimate with you as our spirits are intimate, respecting you as I respect my ideal. Never to profane one another by word or action, even by a thought. Between us, if necessary, let there be no acquaintance. I have discovered you; how can you ever be concealed from me now?'

"One day he will say to his son and his grandson, 'There was a love between us almost bare and leafless, yet not blossomless nor fruitless, a love remembered with satisfaction and security, my love with Mactatotam.' Then he will say, 'I was preserved so long and well, I came to believe no Indian could ever do me harm.'

"Thomas Rolfe moved through the forest, disguised for protection. When he met Mactatotam, sometimes he felt his life had all occurred in his grandfather's twenty-year sleep, dreamt on the long point of departure for America, back there in England where Pocahontas died, Thomas thought, perhaps forever.

"He says to his son and grandson, 'He came in a time of peace and commenced a speech, in which he informed me that some years before he had observed a fast, devoting himself to solitude and to the mortification of his body, that on this occasion he had dreamed of adopting an Englishman as his son, brother, and friend, that from the moment in which he first beheld me, he had recognized me as the person whom the Manitou had been pleased to point out to him for such a brother.

" 'When Mactatotam's tribesmen wished to kill me and eat of my flesh and blood, my friend spoke to save me, a long and moving oration, which concluded, "He is my brother; and because I am your relation, he is therefore your relation too; and how, being your relation, can you enslave him or make the white broth." One of their English slaves cried out, "It is good to bear the yoke in a man's youth."

" 'Then,' Thomas Rolfe said to his son and his grandson, 'something terrible intervened between us. I will not say what, but I dreamt last night of an event which occurred long before. It was a difference with a friend, which had not ceased to give me pain, though I had no cause to blame myself. But in my dream ideal justice was at length done me for his suspicions, and I received that compensation, both punishment and reward, which I had never obtained in my waking hours. I was unspeakably soothed and rejoiced, even after I awoke, because in dreams we never deceive ourselves, we who have fished and hunted and smoked from the tomahawk together, nor are we deceived, and this seemed, this dream, to have the authority of final judgment. Believe this: our truest life is when we are in dreams awake. That my experience confirms.'

"But something terrible had intervened, between the temporal emanations of his voice, between the young man and the old man recalling his youth to his generations."

Drake said, "The Guide, Eagle, Thunderer, Drake, call me any of all the names—I was Pawkittew, the asspriest. I was Pawkittew, the Hybrid, Monkey-guard, Bringer-of-the-stranger. Despite my white, stranger-mother, I knew the figure in the landscape intimately, the woman from horizon to horizon, so naked that she sometimes appeared to me as a man. I knew the conjunction of a sky, which was all sun and fiercely caressing wind, with the giantess of the landscape; and I watched her reveal again, beneath the sky, her secret lushness, known as I moved, a dark figure on her landscape, as I moved into the wind.

"In future days of dull perception, if the figure recedes to the point of disappearance, seldom revealing herself to men, while we only improvise a lushness and a sparseness in her absence; if the wind seems only impish and the sun's resistance seems trivial to us; yet it will be perhaps only for that one time that the secrets are distant, and in my time this is the center of a world and, as yet, the home for human beings, for the people.

"Yet it was also the place I'd been torn from, distortion through the will of the landscape, which had chosen me by my nature, selected me to depart on the mission, away from my people and Sawpootway's. So I returned, achieving the landscape's intention, bringing my treasure, bringing Blau in; and I was pleased to return, after the absence of years spent in seeking the right stranger, waiting to know a white man in the moment my heart moved out from its course, as I saw the boy-man turn in the desired direction and plunge almost indifferently, as if he were already dead, into the western landscape.

"I had appeared first to Berrigan, then to Blau. Now I returned to the place where my two bloods might become almost one blood after my task, bringing a treasure from my priesthood, bringing the young man as my mother was once brought, and others before her, back to the black priest who was the first brought, the priest who was transformed.

"This was the figure, the landscape, I'd always loved, in memory, in its nakedness, for being sparse and lean as my own mind became here—like a double-edged knife as broad as a mirror—the bare flesh of the dun figure under the discovering sun, the fire-rose prairie, the ascendant sun, the scattering of trees along the infrequent unchanneled waters, the coiling scavengers winding the sky above the twisting dust of herds, the dunes that moved sandily, like animals, across the Arkansas, meadowlark, sunflower, cottonwood, the vagaries of the tumbleweeds, and, flushing my face, the husked dry heat of that southwest wind blowing from the dunes, baring the breath of jackrabbit, coyote, rattlesnake, as I moved us, now far from those blue metallic hills, as we approached the Arkansas, coming to the temporary camp where the antelope clan and the time awaited our arrival, confident in my return.

"I opened my mouth to the wind, which coiled like smoke inside, and I sighed, releasing the air through my nose and mouth, riding my gray mule again, emblem of my craft, hybrid on hybrid. I continued to rise before the eyes of the lovers, before the blue eyes and red hair of unsuspecting young Blau, whose preparations for this time had also been intense.

"The division of my blood, which I'd felt so horribly, bitterly, in the years of my absent priesthood, exiled chieftainship, now almost resolved itself in the landscape and in the figured combinations we, as travelers, composed, coming into the Indian camp, which appeared all at once, over a small rise, so suddenly that I heard three gasps behind me, and I smiled, looking back on them, as my mule slid cautiously down toward the river, where I'd already seen the people, the horses, the dogs, the tipis, as yet black figures in the distance, by the shining, curled smoke hovering over a swollen river, near a yellow clump of cottonwood.

"I saw the fear in Marie's face. Berrigan flicked the reins and hugged her joyfully with one arm. Blau sidled his horse toward the front, now hesitating, now coming on, pulling abreast of the wagon, darting forward to see the camp better. I slowed for the young man's approach, rubbed the blue mule's ears backwards.

"Now, as Berrigan's horse floated down the incline in his traces, the gold's momentum thrust him hard forward and tugged on the trapper's trailing pinto's reins, Sawpootway laughed, her face buried in Berrigan's arm, and Berrigan and Blau laughed also in their eagerness, as I led them, still smiling, down. In the village, I saw the faces, coming clearer, of the antelope clan lift toward us. Only the dogs still moved around."

Berrigan said, "Drake said, 'No, don't turn away. You'll offend them.' The antelope clan, the clan Marie came from, was before us, offshore in the river or splashing at river's edge in the broad pools of the wide sandy bottom. All were naked, men, women, children. The children watched their elders without much curiosity and played in the shallow pools, trying to catch fish and frogs in their hands. The men and women seemed seized in a sexual ecstasy that was almost religious. Rhythmically they moved their hands and other limbs and members before the actual penetration, all movements solemn motions of the flesh on flesh.

"Women boldly offered me voluptuous and athletic bodies, but Marie held my arm tightly. Women and men coupled on the sand or, more frequently perhaps, led each other away, disappearing among the yellow trees to consummate their play, as Dutch had already disappeared. He was borne away, on our arrival, by three importunate women after Drake had pointed him out, speaking to the Indians above their increasing shouts.

"Playfully, I set my buffalo hat over a little girl's head. Her head disappeared within the fur, the hat so large, drooping toward her shoulders, that I laughed. Her mother, with obvious signs, offered the girl to me. Marie shoved the woman and girl toward the water, and they went away.

"The Indians seemed to observe obscure boundaries between the private and the public. Their bodies were fully exposed to my view, and they seemed to make a point of exposing themselves for pissing, indifferent to all eyes. The war chief, Tawnew, was introduced to me, and, as he made his sign of welcome, he pissed before us, only turning his penis aside so he wouldn't splash us. In fucking or shitting, the Indians always made some small attempt to hide a part of themselves from foreign eyes.

"The war chief, pissing, seemed also to be bragging, speaking to Drake, indicating, with his free hand, the sky, the earth, the lodges, the corral of horses, the sparse trees, the people, and the river, as if all things were his. Drake, who they called Pawkittew, frowned and spoke sharply in infrequent replies. When there was a pause I asked, 'Is this usual, is it always like this?'

"Marie winced and turned her head away, but Drake said, 'No, this is the antelope clan, and it is not usual even for them.' When I showed no sign of understanding, he said, 'It's like a theatrical. At other times, we say that it is good for one person to be torn from himself but evil for many.'

"Marie had released her grip on my arm, turning her back on the offending scene, her face toward the lodges. Another woman offered herself to me, and I retrieved Marie's hand. Tawnew refused her too. To Drake I said, as the woman left us, 'What about you? Why don't they approach you?'

"Drake said, 'Women don't approach the chief when he's also the asspriest.'

"I'd have said something else, but was startled when I felt Tawnew's hand on my breeches, rubbing my penis through the leather, his grip becoming firmer. I knocked the hand away. The war chief appeared hurt, and for a moment, as his features became confused, I thought he'd cry. I became afraid, having struck him. I pointed to myself and Marie, to our clasped hands, smiling foolishly, trying to show him I hadn't meant offense. The war chief's features realigned themselves against the underlying structure of his bones, and I believed he smiled at me. Relieved, but somehow still frightened, I blurted out to Drake, 'Is there danger that I don't go with the women?' When I'd spoken I knew I wanted to leave Marie's side, wanted to join Dutch in the cottonwood trees, in that minimal or vestigial forest which seemed then so surprisingly lush.

"Drake said, 'Not for you, no danger for you.'

"I noticed Marie was crying, and I found myself angry with her. She must, I thought, have been crying all the time her head was turned to the lodges. 'Stop it,' I said. 'Look, I'm not leaving you. I'm staying with you.' Then she whimpered. She choked and gasped, and I felt foolish and cruel for being angry with her tears. 'What's wrong?' I asked.

"She freed her hand and looked at me, wiping her eyes. She said, 'My father is dead.'

"Against my will, I was angry with all the Indians then. The sun, on the white inner buffalo skins exposed, hurt my eyes, and the glint of silver on the river hurt them. I didn't wish to cry. I kissed Marie, damply, though she was unresponding. The Indians began to straggle away from the river, the show apparently ending. Yet Dutch hadn't reappeared yet, as the sun was declining, making its sunset in the low stratus of the horizon.

"In the dark, I saw two women bearing food from the lodges into the trees west of the camp. They entered the grove where I'd located my envy. I had escaped the tipi where Marie mournfully slept, and I couldn't forget the activities of the Indian women in the afternoon. I wanted so desperately to participate in something of that carnal scene that, tentatively, pretending accident, I exposed my penis, hard on my palm under my thumb, to another passing woman. She touched the tip and made a sign as if meant to convey mock horror at my revealed, purpled instrument. Then she continued toward another lodge, laughing softly to herself.

"As I passed by the tipi where Marie slept as if drugged, toward the campfire where Drake sat alone, I felt my envy of Dutch replaced by a pleasant bitterness I thought I'd like to preserve, at least for the moment. I sat down at the burning buffalo chips to eat some more of the yearling calf. I scorched the meat in the fire, stretched the meat tautly, as my stomach had become pleasantly taut, between my left hand and my clasped teeth, and I sawed off the bites with a flint knife.

"Beside me, Drake sat in silence, and I was as yet too aware of my recent behavior, of my silly exposure to the Indian woman, to speak to him, to ask the half-breed any of the questions I wished to ask. Suddenly I found that I ate in an anger so intensely suppressed that I was holding back tears. I saw Drake observe me, but I was afraid I'd explode if I opened conversation, openly weeping, which would shame me before the half-breed. Questions, not quite formulated, revolved inside my stomach like tiny stone knives bound to a wheel, questions not quite distinct, yet sharp on all edges, protruding in surprising surfaces where least expected, the whirling flint knives, glittering and deadly, and I knew I was stubborn and wrong not to formulate the questions fully, making them explicit between men. I knew that Drake wouldn't likely answer questions I hadn't asked.

"Swallowing the last of my meat, I felt nauseous. The night wind was still harsh and sickly warm on the back of my neck, as if the plains burned on in the dark, as if the darkness were only the black, smoking past left by the prairie fires, marking an irretrievable time which continued to smolder sulphurously, with a sensuous, infective power that was untreatable in the dry land lying flat on each side of the river.

"Tawnew, out of a white lodge, appearing in the firelight, writhing in some special dance like an animal from a nauseous dream, seemed to approach only me. Other Indians closed in, the unfamiliar people looming high above me out of the darkness, surrounding Drake and me. I saw the asspriest's lips set in a hard line and relax again. I understood the motions of the war chief's dance then. His were the motions of the snake handler: revolving arms, body coiled and striking forward, imitating the four thick serpents, the rattlesnakes wrapped upon him like bracelets, violent ornaments, as he exhibited his precise mastery, so apparently careless in mimic exercise.

"Tawnew's eyes shone. His mouth gaped, showing teeth in its corners. His skin glistened with white oil he'd applied. Such a bright human or animal body in firelight, he seemed the consummating image of those random couplings of the river, of the grove, the afternoon. He was so bright he almost cast reflections of himself and Drake in the darting flames, tongues of the fire combining, on the dancer's body, with the flickering, forked rattlesnake tongues.

"Drake rose, darkening my face with his body as he made his first steps. Sinuously, he went forward toward the war chief, in similar dancing, arms before him twisting, while as yet the remainder, torso, of his unpainted body, breech-clothed still, was only slowly walking. He cooed repeatedly, softly but awkwardly, like a bird that has only just found its split tongue. Though he spoke in English, as though for my sake, the words he called I only gradually understood, after repetition, 'Come, my grandfathers, come, my grandfathers, come,' he called, embracing the war chief's bright, slick torso. The four snakes wound themselves now around Drake's arms and wreathed his neck and shoulders, transferring their allegiance, adhering closely to his skin, as if they'd returned home.

"Drake, at last, began to move his torso, hips, his legs, through the contortions of the changing dance, in one definite direction, soon completing his more formal motions, as the dance became more casual, less intense, moving toward the river. Tawnew, as though now excluded by the ceremony, walked negligently toward the white-skinned tent, as if dismissing himself.

"The Indian watchers, men and women, departed, broad impassable faces turning back, features dissolving again in the darkness, while Drake danced away with his calm snakes; while Marie lay in her stupor, mourning her father in sleep; while Dutch occupied himself with love or something similar to love; while I, my nausea returning, throat dry and thirsty, bladder painful, stared into the fire.

"The ceremony had come upon me too casually to comprehend, despite the striking rattlesnakes. The whole scene rose now in my imagination, its fullest significance manifest there, and my mind surrendered its attempt to understand. So I rose, still with questions, and walked, as I knew now I must, to the lodge where Marie lay as if she were dying, where I would watch, sometimes nodding, as my love of her came through the night, where eventually I would sleep, eyes closing of their own accord.

Dutch had not returned to us, and it was still dark. I woke briefly as Marie rose, and I lay down in her place, my nausea bursting, I felt, throughout my body, pouring through my skin like feverish sweat. I lay cold no matter how the sun rose. Each time I woke I stared at the thick hair of the buffalo hanging from the walls, the skins which couldn't warm me anymore. Marie, concerned, no longer mourned her father. As I slept, I felt she watched me now; and I slept well.

"I woke after dawn, just after. Dutch hadn't come and Marie was missing. I retained an incident from my sleep, incident of dream or brief waking, of the half-breed, now called Pawkittew, kneeling in the tipi. He watched me, and traced, as if accidentally, figures in the dust—an eagle, a buffalo, something like an ass, a monkey, a man—each previous figure erased with his hand before the new one was drawn with his finger, each surrounded by what seemed to me the incomplete figure of a fish, unfinished at the mouth so the pattern lay open, as if the pattern were intentionally flawed. What I remembered as he drew was a monkey I had seen in a silly suit, little boy's sailor suit, whirling with open palms among the laughing audience, as the organ grinder played some patriotic air.

"As the incident dissipated, I rose and walked shakily through the tent door, brushing back the flap of fur, into the fresh light outside, where the Indians, beginning to stir, emerged from their tipis. They seemed clearer to me now, more ordinary in dawn light, less sensually exotic. They became occupied with such ordinary matters as feeding themselves and their horses. I thought I saw Marie, briefly appearing, holding up the flap of one of the tipi's, disappearing within. The tipi was Tawnew's, the one he'd emerged from and reentered the night before.

"Some of the Indian women, including the one I'd exposed myself to, spoke to me in a friendly manner. They went on about their work when they saw I didn't understand them. I saw the men caring for the horses. A few of the women had begun to raze tipis, converting the lodge poles into travois. The dogs nosed around the remains of last night's feast, as the preparatory movements of the people increased around them.

"I could see buffalo grazing, unperturbed on the prairie, within a prairie dog town. The squirrel-like ground animals went about their own business, only disturbed by an occasional buffalo rolling on a mound for protection against the flies. It occurred to me then that the antelope clan might not be leaving me, that they might take me along with them. It occurred to me, in my sickness, that I might very well be an Indian captive unknown to myself.

"Weaker again, I reentered the lodge and reentered the buffalo robe I'd slept in after Marie. I must have dozed, restlessly, before she appeared above me, almost naked, dressed only in a kind of narrow leather apron, an inadequate cover beneath the waist. She bent down, and her breasts swung free toward my face. She smelled strongly of the buffalo grease on her body and in her hair. She gave me something hot and sweet to drink from a blue and white glazed bowl. As she supported my head and poured the liquid into my gaping mouth, I felt better immediately, enjoying her comforting presence, the pressure of her breasts, fuller than I remembered them, on my arm, the occasional light touch of a dark nipple on feverish skin.

"When I'd drunk the liquid, I was aroused, so I slid a hand between her legs. Her thighs squeezed it softly. Inside she was warm and wet, and she smiled down and spread her thighs again for the easier access of my fingers within her. Yet she interrupted me then, removed the hand, and sucked upon my damp fingertips.

" 'The others will be jealous,' she said. Her accents had become peculiarly mixed.

"I shook my head. 'No, they aren't interested in me.'

" 'Yes,' she said, 'they will be jealous.'

"I was tired of her flirting. I said, 'I don't interest them.'

" 'Fool,' she said. 'They would be if I let them. You would see. You don't know how I protect you.' She passed her hand through my hair, gently. 'You don't know what would become of you if it wasn't for me. You would see. With teeth and claws they would come after you.'

"I realized then that I was hearing a voice from outside, calling hello. It was Dutch's voice saying, 'Hello, Berrigan . . . It's Dutch.'

" 'Yes,' I said, 'come in.' I looked at Marie, but she made no attempt to conceal her body as Dutch entered with Pawkittew behind him. She continued, sitting by me, outside the robe.

"Dutch said hello. He asked how I felt. He asked if I felt I could travel.

"Marie said, 'He will be well by tomorrow, travel or not travel.' Dutch looked at her. She said, 'There is nothing wrong with him that I can't cure.'

"I believed her and added nothing to what she said.

"Dutch said it was his hope we would travel with the clan a few days, north and west from the river to the meeting with the whole tribe, to remain only till we wished to get on to the southwest. He spoke as if it were a pleasure trip he spoke of, one we'd all enjoy.

"I wanted to say something about my fear of captivity, but I looked at Pawkittew, blocking the exit, and I only nodded in reply. Dutch must have assumed agreement, figuring from my nod and from the silence in the tipi. Pawkittew, who had stood frowning, also nodded then, and he and Dutch were gone.

"Then I felt strengthened enough to touch Marie with determined fingers. 'Do you wish me now?' she asked.

" 'Yes,' I said, nodding again, and she slid, so slippery, into the robe, and crouched low above me, so her hand moved between us, caressing me.

"She said, 'You'll be well because I love you and I'll care for you, and we will always be like this.'

"I believed her again, as her body moved gradually lower, and she moved faster above me. I inhaled the odor of the buffalo fat, relishing what seemed now a fine spice to our activity. My tongue flickered between my lips and teeth, touching the elongated nipples, licking near the crests where her veins ran darkly under the skin. I studied where we met, sighting through her swinging breasts. I rose to meet her thrusts. Her lowered torso slid up and down my chest, and her lips brushed my eyelids. It seemed to me that the fig I'd once envisioned, and the fire purple and dark in the fig's heart, now surrounded us quite casually, as if we had met just often enough this way, and now oozed from ourselves into the landscape, so that the landscape enclosed us like a fig, as if we were the fig's deepest pleasure and the farthest, continuing advance of the prairie fire's wavering informal line, as though we were the crest of our own lives.

"But, as I came, in the very height of my pleasure, an image, a kind of dream, flowed unwilled, undesired, into my eyes, of myself, in my own flesh, watching us from the doorway, watching the hump of us shifting under the buffalo robe, watching us all the time, as Marie's final movements of satisfaction projected our joined bodies, entire, from the top of that skin, as I clutched her now in the dust, and I dug into the earth beneath the tipi, where I heard, in the strange earth medium, as the image of myself at the door disappeared, as I listened to the sounds of whatever beast moved within, sounds like the buffalo thunder of the plains, or like the thudding sounds of our own hearts, a sound, earth-covered, in which I recognized the act as our own act, the unparaphrasable interior of our love.

"I felt as if I'd returned to myself, as she rose from me, as if I'd, unbidden, dissolved in the passing act, in my fever resolved into elements of earth and water, fire and air, as the land we seemed to be in rose. I felt as if I receded into the landscape forever, became its horizons and the close blue and white bowl inverted above the flat land, covering the view, felt the breeze upon the buffalo fat she'd left upon me, felt the terrible wind of her departure, and so I knew once more I couldn't leave her, no matter where she took us."

Someone said, "Briefly, in America, Gerhard believed he'd just sailed all that way to rediscover England, in a round trip to that old World Island that England had come to represent to him, a trim garden for the soul, the enclosed garden tempered with an imported wildness, tasteful wild borders, nothing wild about them at all. The landing, after all, wasn't so very different from an English landing he'd once made.

"Even the animals at first appeared to be the old animals. A bird he could compare to the English robin landed nearby him. He penned it in the language, calling it *robin,* though he must have been aware, upon some more fundamental level, that the American thrush didn't quite belong to him or to England, nor to his German homeland. With some eyes he must have seen the spring-tiding bold, russet-breasted bird of the New World: the panic wings through air, the tilted braking tail, as the thrush came to the branch and twig, the male bird's landed song more wild and beautiful than the birdsong he'd known. With some eyes he must have seen, but he slighted the differences: the eventual recognition of this *other* world must occur against his will. Eventually this bird wouldn't be the chubby English bird he'd determined he saw. What prepared him? Perhaps the language of the island remained so new to him, even after his mother's speech and after his own long residence in England, that it made everything he saw through it exciting, eventually made the new land emphatically new, so that his language, learned first from the mother, was somehow more adequate, less a barrier to America, than a born Englishman's was.

"The adopted Englishman, Gerhard Blau, experienced something similar two days after landing, when, rounding a corner, down an alley, he suddenly found himself alone with an American Indian. The Indian, in white man's clothing, sat upon a step, as if waiting for someone to emerge from the back door of a low building. Immediately, the English words failed Gerhard, and he felt himself off-balanced in the opaque eyes, in the unreacting features he faced in the instant. What he encountered in the darkened lane, at evening, was no savage or salvage, as the language would term him, but something, beyond Gerhard's volition, really irredeemable, too early or too late for the salvation Gerhard's language, or Christianity, proposed.

"For this first immediate moment, before he recovered his now even more precarious balance, Gerhard reunderstood the bird thrashing down toward the branches, braking, or he lost his previous understanding of the bird and discovered an opening ahead that could be explored. He reconsidered both the seacoast and the bird. He almost began something he'd hoped for secretly. For a time he would associate this discovery with his mother, whom he'd felt he might rediscover in the new land, recovering a sense of a personal mission, at one with other men, in Clark's expedition; but her values were too far removed from him in her death, and, even when he continued his journey inland, the Indian remained on the steps, the instant they met still continued, proclaiming in Gerhard something that was not yet Gerhard.

"The Indian gazed much as the mare would later gaze at him, as if almost recognizing him in some undefined way, as the Indian seemed to wait for him to make his move, the Indian's presence stating a definitive difference in their likeness. There was something Gerhard had known only in dreams and in dimly acknowledged aspirations: a sense of alteration, an othering of himself he could never lose again completely, even in the most intimate relations with Indians or any others, men or women; and it was this sense which chiefly drew him out, into America, into the continent he came to feel he had to transform in himself, this sense he thought of later as a horse sense, which kept him from lingering on that seacoast long, there dreaming the interior he must enter to try to discover the man, adult, he felt America wanted him to be.

"Perhaps it was the name *Indian* which was close enough to the sense of things he was developing to weight the scale, to renew the comforts of his chosen tongue, even if the Indies were something already known long before, even if all attempts to merge the Indian on the steps with the already known would ultimately meet failure.

"Gerhard had expected the Indian to speak first, to acknowledge the intrusion, but the Indian, perhaps caught up in some obscure vision of his own, only returned the boy's stare. It was then he saw that which allowed him to recover fully. The Indian, he saw, was simply drunk, staring as if from a great natural distance between men, like some predatory beast lurking in mountain underbrush. Gerhard, frightened, found his tongue and spoke, in what he hoped was a friendly manner. It didn't matter what he said, something about the weather, for the Indian, despite his civilized clothes, apparently didn't understand a word of the language Gerhard had just rediscovered.

"As the immediate perception faded out, faltered and ended, Gerhard wondered for the first time what name Indians gave themselves to distinguish themselves from white men. He raised a hand in hesitant farewell, and tried not to hurry out of sight.

"So he was drawn into the continent: first by a need he felt to rediscover his long-dead mother, her ambitions for him, an ideal dream; then by the animals like the mare and the robin, who seemed to him to appear as if just to study him. He knew they didn't know him, and he was happy being unknown to them. He thought the animals didn't even really recognize themselves, which was to him a preservation of himself among them. Then by the Indian, like a mask of America, a persona of the continent hinted at by the animals, of a play whose name was unknown to him.

"If the Indian reminded Gerhard of anyone previous, he reminded him of his father, on the journey to

Russia, in the childhood obscured by time, as if by the vapors of Siberian snow, rising from the earth to drift and whirl like dust about the two travelers, father and son.

"Then he was drawn by the land itself he became more aware of beyond the first mountains, mountingly aware after that crossing, eventually of the land beyond all else before it, because he couldn't find anything approaching a satisfactory definition of it, except as Indians or animals represented it, though it swarmed with shapes in his imagination, almost at times seeming to yield to his imaginary filling-out, in a plenary definition of fictional personae, of masks moving across it, the landscape which at each further approach withheld itself as if at the last moment, receding as in waves before him, rushing westward.

"America drew him on, inward, like a woman; yet would seem to him, at times more frequently, some kind of strange male animal, or an inextricably male-female one—the new earth and new sky which he called to himself *the landscape*—so he would come to wonder, after the Indian camp of the antelope clan, what it was he believed the landscape wanted of him, this America that sometimes approached him boldly as a man might approach a woman he knows well.

"In Kentucky, a backwoodsman and a Cherokee took him into a cave to see the huge white bones of the vanished animals, which, according to the Indian, had ranged that country until recent years, which still grazed down mountains far to the west. Gerhard felt and saw a vision of great, hairy elephants, moving long-tusked inland from the Atlantic, faltering at this point, losing hope, falling whitely down dark mineshafts, vanishing; while he, Gerhard, continued through the forest toward mountains where the elephants were only rumored, penetrating farther than the elephants, for all their trumpeting and convoluted trunks and tusks, as if he became, at this point, a transformation of the extinct mammals.

"The frontiersman told him of the gathering on Corn Island, so he continued, in communication with the other he was becoming, into the other country animals and something like animals would shock him into, after a death or two, in the active love between distinguished genders, always alternating, changing through him. Yet he felt as if he still stood before the Indian in the alley, or just moved away, nervously, now. He heard his slowed footsteps in that passage, slow steps though eager, as yet reluctant before the drunk Indian. Gerhard almost faltered, when he remembered England as the only other place America reminded him of.

"In the Indian camp, he remembered, as he rose from the four women, satiated, remembered as he listened to the meadowlark's precise wild prairie song, its simple variations, seeing the bird's flash of yellow under the sun of that dawn, seeing the stippled brown center of the sunflower surrounded by the yellow fan of petals, in the dawn remembered the only place America reminded him of any more: the land of the reindeer people and those other herdsmen, of the squat long-haired ponies, the distant eastern peoples of Siberia. He felt that the difference between that cold East of his father and this heating-up West he was transforming or was being transformed by was only the difference between his childhood and his adult life.

"Gerhard's comparisons soon faded before the sight of Orcus Berrigan in the tipi. Orcus seemed withered in unnatural shadows of the tent of hides, shivering beneath the buffalo robe with the naked Marie, who had just lain with Gerhard, at his side. The man had lost much flesh. He rose on an elbow so whitely, so totally exposed, if the tipi fell aside, to the unfamiliar sun they had both approached.

"Gerhard, in contrast, felt almost alive again, despite the disturbance Marie had caused inside him, after what she had done with him, after the multiple incursions upon the women in the cottonwood grove. He stared at the opposed horns on Orcus's buffalo hat, and felt the landscape's presence under the hides."

Three

Drake said, "This is the night the

fawn is throttled, good eating for men who're despairing of their mission in life. It is February twenty-fifth, and I continue my story, the history of my ancestors, which I don't plan to complete in this passage to Vincennes. I tell it to Blau and Berrigan only. I have begun, as my time runs out, to watch Blau closely.

"A white woman flew above the gray ocean, pursuing an escaped husband, her long white neck uncoiling thickly, her curled beak thrust forward, determined. She appeared in America. She was my grandmother, Hannah Rolfe.

"Picture this scene: a small frontier settlement in the forest, the improvised scattered buildings miles apart from each other, the roughly cultivated fields. Hannah Rolfe's husband, my grandfather, Roger, marked, in his field, a row with his stick, in the very first days of springtime. Seven children, including my mother, played near a brook. A European apple grew by the door of the cabin. The field, in which Roger Rolfe divined the future grain, divided the cabin from the brook, and the horse, tied to a stump, grazed between the field's margin and the water. In the cabin, my grandmother nursed the newly born son.

"You see, it was all so idyllic: a peaceful industrious white man preparing to work the fruitful soil; his children at play near gentle waters; the fruitful white woman absorbed in the new child of such a marriage; even the animals peaceful in the single example of the grazing horse. Yet if you had been there and looked closely, you'd have seen that the house was not built to last. It was just something thrown up that could come down, an improvised walling against something else, as if the builder knew that life couldn't last. Roger Rolfe was its builder.

"There was something temporary about all his

doings, something I like, something uncalculated, to the moment sufficient, as if he were only trying to make the most he could from the irretrievably bad situation. Hannah wasn't satisfied with the improvisatory life. With this newest child in her arms, she was already yearning for places they'd left behind.

"The Indians entered into the improvisation, between the potential cornfield and the leaning shelter, through Rolfe's meager defenses. The Indians were Christians too, of a sort, descending out of Canada where they'd been converted by the French to Catholicism and rum. Only the liquor had burned their throats and bellies going down. My mother suspected the three men among them were drunk, as she gathered her impressions from the brook.

"She fled with her conscience-stricken father, with her brothers and sisters, and with the horse, cut off from the mother and the new child. My grandfather had hesitated before he fled with his seven, perhaps gladly fleeing in his guilt. He fired on the Indians once and missed. Their three shots missed him.

"The three red men entered the cabin, while the rest of them, two women standing just inside the clearing, waited, watching my grandfather, his children, and the horse disappearing. Risen from childbed, one foot bare, the child in her arms, Hannah Rolfe was guided almost gently through the door, when the baby began to cry. The men were angered. One of them snatched the child and swung him by a tiny foot, smashing the bare head open against the apple trunk. Hannah Rolfe cried aloud to her God, as she'd cried silently before.

"She suffered a long journey, an uncertain march into the dark wilderness northward. She resolved to show herself obdurate to the men, but they never approached her in the way she feared they would.

"She did think that dream was about to come true in the Indian camp they came to, where they found two women, an old man, seven children, and one white English captive, a boy. The latter had been a captive for two years, he told her. There, in that northern camp, the men did touch her, to remove her clothes. The four women distributed the clothes between them, putting on the white woman's garments in delight.

"When Hannah was naked, they tied her to the rough bark of a sugar maple, gazed at her, and spat on the ground. For only an instant she assumed a fainting posture before them, then she recovered her obstinacy, an attitude, a honed quality far beyond her thirty-three years, a file-like abrasiveness of will.

"She concentrated on the coldness in the air, the bite of the early spring wind against her white flesh. She fastened her mind on the rough bark against which she'd recently writhed in the simulated swoon, wood which still pricked her flesh. Blood had emerged upon her buttocks, spine, and shoulders. Despite the blood, I think the tree must have suffered more. She concentrated on the blood in her mind, attached her will to all the discomfort she could find. She was dissatisfied when the Indians released her from the tree, binding her feet, her hands behind her. The man who did it, she said, was too careful not to touch her, as if he were constrained by the hand of God.

"In the early morning light, the Indians made her run the gauntlet. Men, women, and children, even the English boy, all brought the clubs down upon her. She fell beneath the blows, but continued to resist until she'd come through. She never lost consciousness, and the Indians admired her for it.

"They gave her a blanket, throwing it down before

her, so she was able to cover the white flesh she believed God protected. I believe that her flesh, from which a child had recently been born, repulsed them, her soft, white flesh, relaxed by the eighth child. Yet her flesh seems to me as hard or harder than it had been with child, as if she retained the child within her, unreleased, unexpelled, like a stone pit around which her body was forming, under the blows, a shell of similar substance, hard within the soft and glistening illusion. I believe the Indians were both attracted and repulsed, for the white flesh was ambiguous to them and almost sacred. I knew they never touched her again. The stone instruments intervened; their own instruments of war and peace turned against them.

"The English boy had never tried to escape in the two years he'd been captive, and when Hannah first proposed it, he resisted, saying it was good for a man to be a slave in youth, to bear the yoke of other men. She didn't yet propose all she intended: only the escape at first, not the deaths she wanted, her revenge on the serpent. I don't know what moved the boy, so previously unresistant to those demons from Canada, to join her in her mission. I've been led to believe he was infected with her, as with a vision, that he came to see himself as the protector of that flesh, a substitute for the husband who'd fled her. My mother said Hannah hinted at something of that nature.

"You should remember I'm not making any of this up. I have to surrender it to you in the way I found it, as it came to me from my mother in my youth. So I tell you that I was told that my grandmother asked the boy what was the best way to kill the Indians, so the slave asked his Indian master to teach him how best to kill and scalp. He said he now wanted, having seen this white woman, to remove her kind from the earth.

"I don't believe the next part of the story. It doesn't seem right to me, not fitting, that the Indian trusted these renegade notions completely, that he suspected nothing in his slave. Supposedly he even pointed to his own temple in illustration of the kill, prophesying his own death at the boy's providential hands; but I believe my ancestors live within me and in this story, so I invent only what I have heard from them. So I have told you.

"When the boy returned from his master, he said to his new mother, bride, or mistress, to the white woman he would join in the act, as he lay his forefinger upon his right temple, 'Strike them there.' He showed her how the lifting of the hair would be performed so well by her, though she was hasty.

"The Indians, of the story, slept so conveniently that night that the woman and the boy rose unwatched before the dawning, and the boy struck his master in the temple with the master's own tomahawk, while Hannah seized a similar weapon and struck and struck with that hatchet, her revenge cutting through the conversion of the savages who had always been for her lost souls.

"The woman and boy scalped them, almost all. One squaw ran away through the woods with a favorite boy child. Hannah saw them run. Frightened, she dropped her bundle of scalps. She ran with the boy to the water, and released all the canoes but one which they took as their own, to return down the river.

"Then she remembered that scalps fetched a bounty. They returned to the dead people, took up the scalps, and returned to the boat, the scalps tied together with a piece of Hannah's petticoat; for she'd taken her clothes from the dead bodies of three women.

"They escaped as if by miracle. They met no roving bands of Indians. The white mother and her determined protector were borne down the river, through the forest habitation of animals. They saw few signs of the past presence of any kind of men. Once there was an Indian graveyard, once some tree stumps.

"They returned to the settlement. My mother claimed all nature seemed to know, in the opening spring, what they had done. Hannah Rolfe returned home with the boy, and the family reassembled: the father with his children, the returned victorious mother, the new protecting son to replace the lost son. They talked like birds newly discovering tongues, singing beneath the leaves now appearing on the apple tree.

"My grandfather leaned against the thin, but burgeoning trunk, as he dreamed, I think, of other women; but he was proud of the wife who'd saved him from himself, and he must have welcomed the new boy, the protector, though fearing sometimes the steel-blue glint in the new son's eyes. The dead child seemed almost unmissed, he'd died so young.

" 'So,' my mother said, 'this is what Eve has come to down the ages: the serpent's proper enemy, and to her seed in that boy, come to a new, American variety of killer, now a whole history of women old before their time, as if at a tea party gossiping. From Eve in the Garden to Noah's wife at the deluge in a single great leap, through ancient monarchies, through Babylon and Thebes, all stages on a journey, breathing awhile at the building of Rome, continuing down through Odin and Christ to—America. And in these stages taken together, I see old women holding hands, a whole circle of tea-drinking ladies, for even my mother became such a one, whose gossip is our universal history, respectable ladies after all. And Eve is only sixty old women from myself, spanning the generations, bearing the generations within them, the hard seeds. Why, the fourth old woman from myself suckled Christopher Columbus; the ninth was alma mater of the Norman Conquerer; the nineteenth the Virgin Mother of Jesus; the twenty-fourth the Cumaean Sibyl; the thirtieth was war-breeding Helen; the thirty-eighth Queen Semiramis; the sixtieth was the Dream of Adam, the woman of the rib, our Universal Mother; and it will not require a very great granddaughter of hers or mine to come in on the death of time, inside our America.' "

I ate of the buffalo meat the four women brought me in the cottonwood grove, reposed between the women as they whispered together, while they giggled their female pleasure. The grove was like an island in the plains, but the other islands I could remember were so different from this one. I lay out of the heat which had begun to come to the prairie, as if embowered in my soul, and only old memory now disturbed the peace, pierced my present as if blades of grass beneath me entered to mark me, severing my soul.

The first island I remembered was the oldest one, the first my mind settled on. It was just the paved, triangular enclosure of my childhood in the city. I played at ball in the interior court, behind the house walls, such musty, vine-eaten walls of my memory. My mother, her ankles lying on a stool, sat stitching her own designs into some garment I would wear.

I threw the ball of red cork against the wall, relished its rhythm in my throwing and retrieving, relished the bright moving ball in the run-down courtyard. Between the three crumbling walls, the place seemed so fresh to the child I was, as if the ball's glow lit the world I lived in. There were, beneath my running feet, weeds in the margins of the huge flat stones, a miraculous good growth. The dirty pool lay displaced toward one angle of the walls. I reached into the pool for the fallen cork bobbing on the scum, and I saw large golden fish in the clouded depths, as Mother presided, the queen of my court, as she stitched under the canopy of her falling, fair hair.

From the grove, I remembered the populous imaginings of my days and nights, of yard and bed; for the distant real children had disappeared from the remembered scene. Surrounded by the curious phosphorescence of the walls in decay, in the heatless brilliance, in the mathematics of my court, at midday, I stood alone, real children forgotten as Mother disappeared into our own wall or house. I could remember, instead of children, the serpent, the witch, and the wolf.

The serpent I felt to be secret and hidden, coiled in the earth beneath the stone slabs, trembling the weedy margins. I saw the witch once at a distance, borne on the shoulders of soldiers, above the housetops. I sat on the footstool paralyzed until her danger passed.

I heard the actual tread of the wolf, would always remember kneeling, innumerable times, at the footstool Mother would leave in the courtyard. The stool had belonged to my dead grandfather. There, in his life, he'd rested his right leg's obscene stump, twisted like a corkscrew in an accident of war. There I closed my eyes, in the absence of my mother, my father on his perpetual journey somewhere else; and I called tensely, whispering in fear that someone else would overhear the words meant only for the wolf, called out swiftly, the words of my ritual, "Come, Wolf," called him to awful protective eminence, "come, wolf, come," my voice slowing through the calls; and my wolf unmistakably did come, though I would never peek from my screwed-up eyes, came with the recognizable tread, the limping walk of my dead grandfather. The world took its mysterious and obscene turn, as the animal entered the courtyard from sky or pool or walls. Then he passed into oblivion and silence, as I released myself, happy that the dead figure had come once more into my life. Pleased with my power, I was relieved to see, after it all, the familiar backyard, to hear the reassuring clicks of my mother's beads in the house. I put my hand on the latch. I entered her house.

Before the journey to Scottish islands and the storm at sea, there was the English island, the war-time clamor of mercantile London, a new England rising sootily from the green ashes, as I worked my double trade in the streets. The green ashes, as if wind-disturbed, themselves rose upward more distinctly for the gray cloud, composing the image I most retained in the grove, as I turned away from the London banks, in whose shadows I'd labored, to an English country garden which became the key, turning image of my long British sojourn, the large garden owned by the aged lord whose useless hanging guns I refurbished, who I led wandering on the Scottish journey, my employer and friend, whose own language I felt returning there in the cottonwoods, intruding into my present rushes and expulsions, through the afternoon and evening, toward the dawn, as I lay in exercises of love.

Some of his language returned, and the man, in memory, returned, the continuing presence of Sir

Robert, Captain Wilson's elder brother, who I thought I'd surrendered to my dead, the self-confessed minor poet who, for many years had suffered, through his garden, a desire for what Scotland meant to him. "I am," he said, "after all, only a poor imitator of that Scot, James Thomson, and I am one who has never seen Scotland." He suffered a desire, he said, to discover the origin of Thomson's poetry, to separate out and discover in Scotland some basis of his own for original verses, while he yet had time.

His concern had entered his garden, which may have been his one most significant work of art, the landscaped garden where a marginal wildness had been introduced, a studied wildness from surrounding woods and meadows, from gentle brooks, a wildness associated with the boundary of Scottish mountains he'd seen in books or heard about from travelers. The English lord dreamed of Thomson's Scotland, never hearing the wild tales his own wandering brother told him except in a kind of translation. He dreamed, through Thomson's Londonized Scotland, the unseen northland, transformed the land he owned. I thought the character of the transformation very English: his appropriation of the wild underpopulated country as if that wildness didn't prove so really wild after all, in his dreaming, as if that other country had no existence except its English existence.

Meanwhile the garden signified an as yet indefinite alteration of his consciousness, a meaning as yet unassigned, in the appearance of distant landscapes more sublime and less human in the waking mind of the poet-farmer, his very peculiar articulation, in the garden, of both nature and artifice, of natural artifice and artificial nature, which I admired, wishing to be thoroughly English; though I was dissatisfied with an England too close to my own past, and I admired the garden despite a mechanical element I thought I perceived in the overall design, of the city's sterling hand, suggesting hatred and contempt for that foreign place in the island, which implicitly opposed the vacant landscapes Sir Robert imported over the terminal northern mountains, over the Cheviots.

The garden was England for me, and there I became, in its careful island, almost an Englishman, if too foreign by past or future, yet appropriated, like Scotland, by the language I learned there, turning the city streets behind me.

In the grove, it felt good to return, if still in memory, to America, as if America were something to be remembered, good to return over the gray quarrel of the water, coming into the gathering on Corn Island again, to the harvest of the colonies, where the men I remembered seemed so different from the four women present in the grove. I wondered whether, if Cantrell should suddenly appear in the grove, instead of on Corn Island, I would wish to protect the women from him.

Unresolved, I recalled the men playing cards, moving their limp cardboards, plying the numbers and courtly faces—four courts: clubs, diamonds, hearts, spades; two tools alternating with two treasures—while Cantrell spoke and the men nodded. Smith and Thomson played their cards on either side of him, separated from their collusion only by his physical presence.

The men had spoken, in halts and rushes, of western lands they hoped one day would turn beneath the plow, land they might acquire by their approaching expedition. They'd seen themselves, within the rhythms of the cards, precursors of a white, most human, tide, bravest forerunners of an almost religious achievement; but now Cantrell spoke the common desires, even my desire as I'd joined them, even as he distinguished himself, with slight indications, from the rest of us. He reminded us we all were hunters of the ideal.

"For myself," he said, "I have no use for plowing, never have. But men like us have got to prepare the way for plowing, making possible the clearings for the future, for the use of farmers, maybe even ourselves becoming the farmers some day. When farmers come, men like us will build the roads among the farms, and we'll be the militia to protect the new settlements. And we must have schools then where our children may learn to preserve the heritage. We must have laws, which are the safety of our women, our mothers and wives. And we've got to have the women themselves to keep our civilization safe. And the young must learn our laws, and we must ourselves learn to obey them, coming to understand that the laws are what are best for even us, those rules we have agreed on in common. We have got to have courthouses and even jails. We've got to have churches certainly, certainly churches; surely you can understand it. And we must understand the importance, now, of what we're doing here." Cantrell paused, his head bowed as if in thought as he studied his cards. The men remained silent around him.

In the grove, I tried to remember if, for certain, he'd believed what he said. On Corn Island, I struggled to grasp the cause of enmity between Cantrell and me. From our first meeting there had been something which almost made me disagree with what he said, a collision of two persons as if from original sources or as if shaped by some unforeseen future event.

I could almost overhear, in the cottonwoods, what

Cantrell had said, the precise sound of his voice while my own lips moved slightly, my remembering lips, as I remembered how he'd resumed, as I hastily bit hard into the buffalo meat the women brought me.

"For myself," Cantrell repeated, "I don't wish to plow any land just yet, though the day comes, I know, when it's time for all of us to settle down, with a wife and children, to settle to their protection, determining to extirpate any species of varmints that plague them. So preachers wander so far this way, to bless the future homes and root out evil in the beginning of settlements, ere many of our women come to these backwoods."

Once more the captain paused before concluding. They sat between hands, and no one was dealing another. One of the men at Cantrell's side, either Smith or Thomson, yes, Smith with the longer face, I remembered, said, interrupting the silence, "We got to have preachers come from ourselves. We got to preach ourselves." I remembered him, Smith, and remembered Thomson, but I didn't wish to pity men.

Cantrell continued as if he hadn't heard, "Yes, you've got to turn the soil over to make it produce, and you've got to make certain it's your soil, and keep it, and you've got to preach from the turned soil and save what can be saved, and not waste your substance on worthless things; to make a place where women can come, bringing that refinement we resist too much. So this is why you're here. This is why I'm here. To open the land to future generations. But no farming for me yet, I'll tell you. Because I've got to be out past the frontier, either carving a road or a clearing, a volunteer man, preparing for settlements, and what we obtain in this mission, ordained by God, none will take away from us."

We nodded our solemn agreement, as the cards circulated again, ringing the blanket in small piles of five. Then vague and dreamy, we responded to a new voice intervening; for the colonel himself had appeared among us, as was his custom, adding to our dream.

"Those men," he said, "you have seen in the Kentuck clearing, yourselves and men like you, men who have brought their families and livestock over the barrier that held us back too long, these ennobled people will one day, not too distant, follow our lead into the land we enter tomorrow, into a land so fertile future crops will all but grow themselves, at just the touch of their human hands. In the same way all nature collaborated with our common ancestor, with Adam who was, as we know, a husbandman. She yielded to him before he fell out, foolishly, with his God. Let that be a warning. It is the New Paradise we prepare for our race, for the new race of free men. For what will constitute this New Eden? For who else shall be that New Adam? Why, it will be freemen on free land, earned through their labor of love with the land. Who else but the yeoman, a natural republican, democratic, moral, and free, from the nature of the land itself, men as broad and fertile in their souls as the valley of this river, on land apportioned equally among equals, each yeoman tilling just as much as a man and his family can till, not more nor less. Can you imagine the children of men like these, sturdy yeomen as you'll be, yet men better than we currently can be? Why, children greater than ourselves, increasingly greater too, in each succeeding generation; for they will settle the promise on themselves, proceeding into the future confidently. They will settle the promise we give them. Look to your future heirs, and see them living in a land without slaves; for the nature of the land forbids men to have or be slaves. In that future land men will not be slaves and the sons of such men will not be slaves. There will be no rich plantations in iniquity and inequality, owners enslaved to those who slave for them, not from this land we enter, no, nothing but free men, yeomen who are always the strength of a great nation. These united communities, from the Alleghenies to the Mississippi, yes, even, I believe, to the far great mountains, eventually; for it is all the one great basin, the heartland of the nation, to which the Mississippi is the great artery. This is the promise of the land to you and to your progeny. This is the reason we embark on this mission."

And we were moved, and we went about our final preparations like men in a dream. Oscar Smith, so long-faced and serious, helped me pass out the guns I'd readied. Packer Thomson stood around with his hands in his pockets, watching us, not knowing what to do with himself to help, with hands or feet, till we came to checking the boats. Then he told me how his father had come to this continent as a young man, as I had. I wouldn't pity them, I thought in the grove. Berrigan came to the tiny bay and watched us silently, as I checked the bateau, the other boats I'd organized construction of. Then, without a word, he went about some other work, to return carrying supplies. I wondered what he thought.

We worked much like the yeomen Clark promised we'd be, our hearts, I think, nobler by the common cause, working steadily, captivated within his vision of us, already moving, in our hearts, through the Garden of the Rivers, centered on the meeting of Ohio and Mississippi. The potential garden spun out, a silken web from that center, unwinding from the dream of ourselves, as we were propelled by the dream of Clark from Corn Island; and I remembered, in that setting out, my mother in the old land behind me, in the past, remembered most her constant concern for my future, as if she knew she would soon die; remembered how I'd come to love Clark as my new father, who my mother had always sought, the father my mother designed with her busy needles, father she told of in the prayered pattern of her beads, clicking them, needles and beads, together, implying an impalpable presence which seemed about to materialize in her time, presence becoming in all time only the instants of the eternal, democratic day we entered, over the falls, in the black sun on the river.

As the dark was coming, a fifth woman entered the grove; but, from my memories, in the green and yellow bower of consolation in the barren plains, I rose to the fourth woman. She stroked my genitals, recalling me to a present life. The movement that had brought me into Clark's dream had itself thrust me beyond his democracy, far from my mother's dreams and love, into a life like my father's, into an intense remembrance of his old life in my present one, the individual male among an alien people. I looked at the surface of her eyes and features, as she lay, apparently unmoved, beneath me, and I believed that everything I'd killed in me had been becoming my father for a long time, or becoming something, past Clark's dream, that was like my renounced father, as if I'd been an American from time's beginnings, in an America indifferent to my urgent thrusts into the woman. Orgasm was a shock I felt occur outside me, past her, an explosion as of the sun going down the horizon, as it did, like a rainbow in the stratus and cirrus, as if my seed, thrust to the horizon I could barely see through the trees, cast a light back through the low clouds of the early evening, cast through the plains dust to shake my flesh with an external force.

The woman, when I'd done, seemed more than ever an indifferent mass of inhuman flesh, unable or unwilling to share my natural existence. Yet when she rose from me, she smiled so broadly and seemed so filled with a joy, as if she'd conceived a peculiar idea of me of her own, which she could no longer suppress. She appeared to struggle within herself to contain that joy, lighting the other women as if with her body, as her pleasure modestly escaped her. And I thought she had desired that escape.

The other women returned her smiles. I peered at the horizon through the women and the cottonwood trees, the sun as if in her rapture over there. An individual strength, more forceful than before the act, returned, as she reminded me of something in Marie, something now so close to me, folding in, something I preferred farther off, there with the sun dipping beneath the horizon.

The women left the grove some time after it was dark. Though emptied of desire, when the fifth one seemed to linger I reached out toward her. She hadn't come near me before, and now she backed away, her fingers spreading her labia, as if to display, despite the darkness, the layers and the depth. She disappeared with the other women, east of the trees, toward the tipis.

Then I also wished to depart from the grove, following the path five women had taken, women whose motives, I reflected, were utterly obscure to me. I didn't see anyone. I came to the river and bathed my body languorously, and still felt I had the odor of the women and of myself upon me.

I woke, in the early dawn, within Marie's body. I'd entered her sleeping, while I was unknown to myself; and I woke feeling dimly a lingering dream of exotic languors, the slow and soft dream of recent events in the grove, and my seed flowed into her smoothly, as if from my dream, while I framed her now fuller body with my slender one. I felt I passed through her in my seed, and that my relinquished seed returned to me: passed through Marie's body, merging with her to emerge, and, after a reformation of my flesh, drove also through the sun—as yet, behind the trees, unseen but warming—my seed pulled unwilled from me, my body dissipated through hers, reassuming myself beyond her as though I had become my own child; passed, my whole new self dispersed into the veins of the sun, achieving another new formation beyond; so that I stood behind the light, before the process, as if doubling on its own extension, returned me.

I found myself again, with Marie beneath me, the new self discovered in the solace of the grove, returning to my life, slippery through things, through worlds of sun and woman, firmer now I'd passed the act than before it, as though the sky of plains, wind, sun, had simultaneously burned through Marie and locked into me in the grove, like my seed returning to the begetter. I became full with the life passing to me through her, as though all had risen and fallen in the single movement—the same direction, the same moment—on a single thread that doubled my existence.

I found her then so much like one of the recent women, afterwards like women of the previous evening. I felt no shame that she was Orcus's woman, nothing more than a small shock of memory, recognition and slight regret. I felt I'd entered my life from behind like a thief of myself.

Marie continued to hold me as I turned aside, one breast lying heavy against my right eye, her body pressed upon me to the hip. She had lifted her knees toward her breasts, lay with an arm around me, one hand down on herself. She seemed to hum, in her body, in our contact, a murmur of the flesh; so I heard the organized sounds, the words she formed lazily with her lips, before I realized she had spoken to me.

She repeated what she'd said, her body's vibration against mine signifying something other than complacency. She said, "Now I will have your child to give Orcus Berrigan."

I disentangled myself from her arm and raised leg. "My child?" My voice, replying, sounded to me as if it were changing between the two words I said.

"Yes, he will be a very special child to me, my child and the child of He-for-whom-we-seek-life. Now I'm glad I didn't conceive of Tawnew; for now I will have this kind of child, and not even the asspriest will know who he is." Her voice ended on a note as of revenge.

"I don't understand," I said.

"It doesn't matter if you understand." She sat up, laughing, and I saw the clutch of grass she'd held between her thighs. She threw the grass away and lay down again beside me. "You won't speak of this," she said. "It will be a secret between us." When I just looked at her, she continued, "You mustn't ever tell Orcus Berrigan, or speak of this to the war chief or the asspriest, not to any of my clan, not to the tribe. For the child, you must promise."

There wasn't anyone I wanted to tell about it. "I do," I said, "but I never wished for any such child."

"If you haven't, then you should be told that such children are not to be wished for. They only come as gifts, by unwishing them, as I have done and will do."

I said, "You mean, like your parents did with you?"

"Perhaps," she said, "perhaps." Her fingers moved, thoughtfully, upon her belly. She said, "It is the last thing I can do for my people."

I believe then that what she intended was a secret salvation of her tribe, in her invented conception and ritual of our child. I thought I understood, from various gatherings in various times, that I had been chosen by Pawkittew, by the asspriest, for some purpose signified in the name she'd called me by, He-for-whom-we-seek-life, to be the bearer, somehow, of some necessary life, perhaps their own future life, as though they all expected to die. Marie, I supposed, had chosen to work both with and against their purpose, developing the confused rudiments of her own morality. Now she insisted she herself bore that life within her, seizing my life from my sleep, exquisitely, waking me up to her scheme. Suddenly I felt the potential sorrow of Orcus strongly, for I felt he must be her permanent lover, so I asked her, "What will become of Orcus, with you, if he's not to know this? What kind of future would you give him this way, if you have my child?"

Her features became very grave. She said, "I alone am his future. He hasn't another. He may have nothing, except through me."

So I saw more of her scheme, of what was for her a religion, the ligaments that now held her life together. I tried to think of something else to talk about, something that might even deny the reality of everything we'd just done and said, but I surrendered that effort, seeing its achievement undesirable.

There was also something even in me, in my rejection of her aim, that wanted her conception to be true, wanted a child from her body to be also from mine, and, knowing, I thought then to say, "Now do you become an Indian woman again? Do you become Sawpootway again, like when you were a child, hidden in the bushes? Do you become, from this, the antelope-child?"

She was frowning as I spoke. She said, "Here and there, only for some moments can I be one of my people. Now I'm nothing in myself. I believe that's the way it is now. Now I shall serve the child only."

And I asked her again, "But what of Orcus Berrigan?"

She surprised me then, for her frown disappeared, and she smiled softly as she said, as if she were a child again, the smile and voice innocent and native, "Oh yes, I shall love Orcus Berrigan." She kissed me lightly, leaning quickly away. She said, in the same way, "And he is your friend."

She spoke the last word loudly, and I glanced around afraid to see anyone in the grove. Only a lone jackrabbit squatted, observing us, some distance through the trees. His long ears trembled as if to the vibration of our voices. Marie seemed to shiver against me. In my own breast a continuous if subdued shudder came, and I felt suddenly tender toward Marie, touching her gently to feel the coupling of our pulses, the pulse and repulse like the doubled thread, so separate and so close, our hearts beating through my life in the grove. It was both a remembered and a present rhythm, as though the rabbit, antennaed, conveyed to us our recent act, in this aftertime, as if that rodent dissolved the interim and now my heart was the receding landscape's shudder, present definitively in me. I'd imagined that landscape so often, so often improvised it. I imagined Marie was tender too, as she came closer under my encircling arm, and I'd become so aware of my own heart, heard it, how it sustained my life. Never again would I ever be able to take my own body and the body's life for granted, feeling as if I had died and that my death continued in my new life as an alternate rhythm.

Then I laughed, and the rabbit ran, dispelling that

temporary scene of Marie and me tender together. The scene repulsed in the rabbit, I knew I was jealous of Orcus, and that Marie loved not me, but only my potential child in the fulfillment of her scheme, in the obscene religion. Since I was chosen, I wished that she loved me, beyond any kind of children.

It was when she frowned again, turning eyes down from me, showing only her lids in a sadness I couldn't penetrate, that she told me, "I will help Orcus Berrigan away from here. He would die here, with my people. He would die now with his own people. We must promise him something else."

I couldn't think of anything to console her. I didn't understand quite what she meant. I'd become aware of our odor, of the buffalo fat which was her only adornment, the newly assumed dressing; and I remembered the talk we'd had as we lay together before, at the spring near her husband's cabin, remembering my own foolishness, and I said now, "What kind of creature will you be then, wherever you'll go with him?"

"Nothing," she said, "but the woman who loves Orcus Berrigan, not Indian woman, not white woman, only the woman who serves the child."

So I insisted once more on her lover, "And what of Orcus Berrigan, what life do you wish for him? If you serve my child?"

"He will be the man who loves me, who also serves the child from He-for-whom-we-seek-life; and we will have our own life then, and other children of our own flesh, and even this child will be of his body, as soon as I go to him."

Then, in that moment, she seemed only silly to me. I wondered if I ought to tell Orcus all about it, right away, and let him do what he liked with us, tell him what I'd done with the woman I knew was his own. But her frown had turned into tears, and, inexplicably,

I thought of the death of her father, Snakesnorter, so I told her, "Marie, tell me about your father." I said, "Will you talk about him?"

"Yes," Marie said. "Would you listen to me?"

I said, "Yes."

"There's not much," she said, "and I'm ashamed to cry for so little."

"Go on," I said. "Then tell me the little."

"He died at this place waiting for you, grown old in a day, they say, dying in a moment. They say they didn't see him die. I don't mind so much that he dies, for he was very old and must have suffered much in the swift aging; but my own clan will not tell me, they say they don't know, where he lies. I don't believe them. They say he wandered away alone, so they wouldn't eat him for his holiness. They say they searched for him. They said they couldn't find where he was, and they're lying to me. So I cry when I remember the lies."

I said, foolishly, "You've always cried. You shouldn't be ashamed." She was wiping her eyes when she laughed at me. I said, "Why don't we look for him ourselves? Orcus and I will help. It's simple as that. You see?"

She said, "No, you look with me. He is too ill. I'll only be away from him for a moment. No, I think he's too ill."

I was already on my feet, looking for my breeches because I hadn't heard Orcus was sick. "Why didn't you tell me before; why didn't anyone tell me?" She tied a kind of leather apron round her waist. "What's wrong with him?" I asked her.

Marie didn't answer. She rose and we walked through the cottonwood trees. We passed through the working women who turned from us unspeaking. We approached the tipi and Marie said, "You may look, but you must leave me with him for awhile. I must be alone with him. His flesh must join with ours."

I scarcely heard her. I opened the flap, peering beneath the hide when she'd entered. There lay Berrigan, asleep and partially uncovered, as though he'd tossed the robe off restlessly in dream. Just as she'd said, he looked as if he were about to die. Something had happened to him I hadn't had time to notice before. He was so white and bony, his flesh sagging down into the robe Marie recovered him with.

"Stay away now!" she whispered, signaled me away from them. I didn't understand what she meant. The sight of Orcus's nakedness disturbed me. I wandered back, passing the grove, along the river westward. I thought Marie might be destroying him. In his possible death, I despised all new life in myself or in others. I hated Marie, all she was to me and to Orcus. If I did believe my seed stirred to the life within her now, I thought I might do something more to her, her death to her, or I might somehow cause my child's life to destroy her. I had no idea of my own life any more. Then I no longer believed in her conception, if I ever had. She was too far from me then, becoming too undesirably other.

As I began to wish all the Indians dead, Pawkittew appeared to me from upriver, his face moving between the long ears of the white-blue mule, coming into the sun, and, though I didn't desire the death of Orcus, nor the dissolution of their love, I thought how I loved Marie, more than I knew her.

I followed Pawkittew and the mule to the sweatlodge he'd built, of four cottonwood branches and of buffalo hide. He instructed me how to bear the stone inside and place it on the fire. He'd brought water from the river in the intestines of the buffalo. The air above the river shimmered, wavy heat, as water evaporated swiftly in the hot sun and wind.

We left our breeches just outside the lodge. We poured the water, from the animal bags, out over the stone, concealing ourselves in the vapors, sweating out our journey, purging our flesh. I felt as if the steam gently removed my skin. Pawkittew spoke to the poles, hide, stone, fire, and steam, in the Indian language I couldn't understand.

When we stepped outside again, I felt cleansed, my bare body a cool, moist substance in the dry, bright air. We stood together, drying on the sand. I told Pawkittew about the grove, the five women, asking him what it meant. He said that the fourth woman, named Ootway, believed she had conceived my child. I was so startled, I almost told him about Marie, and I felt I should have thought of what he'd told me, should have realized it already, what the woman had felt. I asked him, "Why was I chosen?" He had his back turned to the rising sun. He wasn't about to answer me. I said, "What if she didn't? What if she didn't conceive?"

He turned and said, "That is the child I must raise to be the new asspriest, which the ancestors will raise to themselves through me, just as I was raised before, and many before me, the children of the strangers."

As I touched my drying stomach with my fingers, my whole body, after the sweatbath, shone around me as if I'd discovered it for the first time. To the southwest, I noticed a purplish cloud had risen and approached, roiled above the wavelike dunes. I said, "The child might die." Pawkittew studied the approaching cloud. I said, "She might be wrong. She might not have the child after all."

The asspriest had begun to dress, so I did. The wind had risen, noisy now, audible in the swirling cloud. Pawkittew said, "If the woman hasn't conceived, she'll be killed by the clan, and they'll eat her for her life."

I shivered, colder than before, though the air had become gritty and more heated; I clutched my shoulders and became warm again. We both stood looking at the sandhills. Hopelessly, I said, "And if the child does die?"

"Then the antelope clan and the war chief will eat the child for its death. The war chief is always of the antelope clan. If the woman hasn't conceived your child—and you must never touch her again—the war chief will triumph temporarily, and I will have to go out from my land again, to choose another, spending myself in the white world again, enduring what has become terrible to me."

"Then I'll stay here and make certain the child lives. I'll just stay here till he reaches whatever age is proper for a new asspriest. I'll stay however long it takes for the child, so no one will die."

Pawkittew said, "If you're here when the child is seen swelling Ootway, the war chief will feast on your whiteness in his solitude, and on the whiteness of the child in the womb, and will taste of the mother's darkness, and of the darkness in the child." I couldn't think what to say then. Pawkittew took hold of my arm. "Come back into the sweatlodge," he said, "till the dust storm passes."

The air had become dark, as the cloud ascended above us like the thronging western locust I'd heard tales of, but this, I understood now, was only the dust the earth, risen up, would fling over us, to cover us as with her dark, outflung arm. I let Pawkittew lead me into the small tent. The image of Clark rose in my mind like the dust, and I knew his dream—of settling noble men, en masse, ennobled by the land—had died in me forever, that his vision had never been quite the truest part of my experience in America. I imagined faces in the smothering cloud, the deadened features of men like Smith and Thomson, as though from their beginnings dead, and more eager faces like those of some of Clark's young men, who I now saw all dead in their too common land, overwhelmed by their earth.

Pawkittew and I crouched in the sweatlodge, near the rock and extinguished fire, our backs to the storm, and I thought again of Marie, and I said, "Why must the tribe eat each other? I don't see why."

"Only the antelope clan eats the human flesh, though they eat for all of us."

"The antelope clan," I mused. I noticed my eyes were tightly shut, and I opened them. "Does that mean that Marie has . . . ?"

Pawkittew laughed. The storm hit the sweatlodge, as if uncountable riflemen fired continuous rounds. Startled when the lodge overturned, I screamed from the shock, over all my hindquarters, of the stinging earth, like the pricks of a million stitching needles. I had sprawled out, and Pawkittew covered me with his body till the brief storm passed.

With his help, I struggled up, ashamed of my weakness, shaking after the storm. He said, "Don't worry so much, not even about your friend who loves Sawpootway. She can no longer be of her tribe or clan, not as she was. She has learned your own language, your ways, just as I have learned your ways from my birth. I speak three of the white man's tongues from my earliest days, taught so much by my mother and the asspriest. And, like me, Sawpootway now has this kind of holiness about her." He looked after the departing cloud. "Now," he said, "we must travel to join the rest of the tribe. The journey will take the remaining daylight, over the plains to the west, north of the river, and you'd be foolish, for your own sake, not to come."

I said, "All right, I'll do as you say." I removed my arm and walked beside him, still stunned, as the mule followed us, unguided. "Why was I chosen?" I asked him; but he didn't turn to me, didn't answer. It made me angry. The time hadn't been so long since Marie rose from my body in the grove, only seemed long now. I said, "Will you protect Marie and Orcus the way you did her father?"

The camp was visible, as we rounded the little bend. He said, "When I was gone, the tribe belonged to Tawnew and to his antelope clan. Until this morning, only Tawnew knew how to find her father. Now I also know, and I'll tell her soon."

"I'm glad," I said. Feeling foolish after my anger, I didn't know what else to say.

"As a white man, perhaps you are right to be glad; but for us, this is the beginning, I think, of our sorrows. Because Sawpootway has become what she's become, and because she is what she once was."

I said, "I don't understand you."

"Let's go see your friend. To see if he's able to ride in the wagon."

So we went to the tipis, and I cried through the hides, "Hello, Berrigan . . . It's Dutch!"

With Marie, I observed carefully the funeral aspect of the death more definite, though similar, than my previous and imaginary death before Caldwell in the ravine. Marie removed the parts of her father from the several holes in the shallow river bottom. I watched while she washed them in the water of a pool, and lay the cleansed fragments together on the buffalo hide, in a semblance of his living proportions.

Pawkittew had guided us there and left us, after Marie had come from Orcus's tent. In the camp, the clan waited for us to finish. Pawkittew restrained their departure, as the sun rose higher.

Marie's hands were gentle on what was left of her father, brushing the sand away into the water, laying the pieces out. Everything was there except the heart and genitals, but his eyes had been put out and the outer layer of his skin had been cut carefully away, in large segments. Everything was so close to my previous vision that I wondered what physical death I would really find in the future—perhaps one of uncomfortable coincidence; the death of Snakesnorter obsessed me more than it had any right to, simply because I'd imagined my own death in its manner, or simply because the old man in death reminded me of my own father, dead in Europe after his travels.

Marie made me remain with her father and, as I saw her disappear, beyond the sweatlodge, around the bend, I could, I thought, reconstruct the shaman's death on the river. He'd been flayed alive, skillfully, the outer skin removed as whole as any skin could possibly be removed, from head to toes. The whole body, still living I thought, had been divided with the knife, in clean incisions, life skillfully prolonged as long as possible, while the members fell from the torso after the bones were broken—all the extensions, of arms and legs, toes and fingers—before the stroke came to the breast. The heart, jerked from his breast, must have palpitated in the killer's hand. The head was swiftly severed with the white man's knife, neither mine nor Orcus's, which must have been in the tribe a long time, despite the blade's sharpness. Death was surely welcomed in the gush from the breast, an eagerly embraced death then.

And there was no brave horse to plunge free over

the western land, only the obscenity of death itself, the dying body lingering in the dying mind, the flesh so raw it must have seemed to bear its whole life outside itself, nervy, too fearfully exposed to things, wounded by each brush with the exterior air, the continuing abrasion of the surface which wears a man down.

And the black birds gathered as I watched, vultures hovering, while Marie was gone so long I thought of going after her. From the air, they examined the spot, the realigned body on the animal skin; so I flapped my arms before my face to let them know I, at least, was still living. Yet they gathered, yet hovered, winding in air, as though static on their long-winged carriages. It wasn't necessary, after the death I'd once imagined, to think much about the shaman's disfigurement; but Marie was so long returning, and it was necessary to consider something besides the increasing discomfort in my stomach. If I'd known how, I would have slept there.

She came back bearing another hide, filled with pouches, one of which she opened to reveal her father's dried skin, a grotesque caricature of a living man. The next pouch contained the freshly-carved genitals. In the third pouch were two fresh eyes and a heart. I almost recognized the eyes, but turned away to vomit, as she uncovered the still damp skin and still steaming bowels. I couldn't speak when I wanted to.

I'd seen more than I had wished to see. I looked toward the dunes of the south, pale multiple breasts of a woman I no longer knew; yet the dunes seemed to calm me, and I watched her again, at first from only the edges of my eyes. It was marvelous what Marie achieved with her two hands, constructing, of the dead members and freshly killed parts, an image of the flesh, as if she knew her father's anatomy by heart and so believed she could wholly restore him, or transfer him whole to another world of life.

When I could speak, I said to her, "Marie, who is it?"

In my ears, a ringing sound, like an audible haze, obscured the background of my own words, making them strange to me; and I could barely hear her say, "These are my father's by right, his members I've returned from the other who took his, this the heart of the other, these the instruments of his power, these the windings of the interior, this the old skin of my father, this the new skin of another life." She stitched at the body she'd made, new skin stretched over the old, with a thong of buffalo gut, her fingers so apt in the task, as though from a life's experience she couldn't have had.

I asked, "Who was he?"

"Tawnew." She studied my face then, and she said, "Tawnew waited on his death. You don't understand, do you? The asspriest must have told you very little, less than he and my people have told me. This death came to Tawnew only a little sooner than the death he expected. My tribe isn't what I thought it was. Things like these have never happened in my own lifetime, and I know little. If you want answers, you must ask the asspriest until he answers. He will have to answer you, if you'll keep asking. He'll have to answer something."

"Yes," I said, "I will ask him."

She'd covered her father's members, mixed with those of Tawnew, within the largest hides she'd stitched together. She knelt back on her heels as she spoke. "It was terrible for me when Pawkittew explained himself, telling me not to tell till we'd come here, told me early on the trail, and I didn't wish to believe his words. They were too strange to me; but I must believe him, and I must believe now what my own clan has said." She smiled. "I also don't understand very well. Like you." She paused, continued then, "It is this. I was a very small child, without memory, when the asspriest left us to live among whites, to find He-for-whom-we-seek-life. To me, until Pawkittew saved Orcus Berrigan, Tawnew was always the chief, and there was no other; just as my father had power, and no one else had other power than what was had through Tawnew or my father. The asspriest was never to be named in his absence. It wasn't proper to name him then. You've seen this." She indicated the buffalo skins, the wrapping at her knees. "When the asspriest returns to us with He-for-whom-we-seek-life, the war chief struggles with him to see who shall live and who die, and who shall then be first among us, war chief or asspriest. It is said that a war chief once won such a struggle, but that time is out of the memory of my people, told in trivial stories, unimportant ones everyone's allowed to hear." She paused. I continued silent. "When my father saw his time had come to die, he left the camp, began walking away. Tawnew followed him to the death, for my father's power. Do you understand?"

"Something," I said.

"When I walked toward Tawnew with Orcus Berrigan's knife, he believed I was the instrument of his death, the hand gods had chosen for the asspriest's victory. He stood apart from the rest, watching their final preparations. He had many pouches on his travois, where the dogs sniffed. He believed it was useless to resist, if the asspriest could use *me*, Snakesnorter's daughter, who had lived with the white men. It was useless, he thought. The other powers were too great for him, he thought, when I told him I'd come to take back my father's life. He didn't move at all. His eyes were like the thin ice on the pools in early winter. I walked straight, and shoved the long blade into his throat. He didn't say a word to me, yes or no, as I whispered whose child I carried, and reminded him whose child I was. He looked at my face as if he'd just remembered me, as if he'd just remembered my name, Sawpootway."

When she lowered her eyes to the stitched skins, I said, "How did Pawkittew know Tawnew killed your father?"

Marie laughed, "Who else would? They all knew. They told him. And Tawnew himself must brag to the asspriest of his new power, must brag and threaten. Tawnew was a fool!"

"What does Pawkittew say of his victory? Of yours, now?"

Her mouth went crooked in its smiling way. She said, "I think he's very surprised. Very little goes to his planning. I'm too much of a nuisance to him. That's what I think."

I'd been digging a hole with my hands, according to the outline she'd made with the old knife, and we lifted the dead Snakesnorter, wrapped in his buffalo skins. We were careful not to disturb the new distribution of his parts, raising him gently, lowering his newly combined flesh, skins within skins. We buried him as if he were sitting up, in the tribal manner. Around him, we placed the signs, which she'd brought from the camp, of his power and prestige: the short bone-bow, the quiver full of his arrows, his long snakerattles—Marie called them shells—the pouch of his medicine. We filled another pouch with dry earth and the matted short grass of these high plains, with the remnant of this plateau in the prairie. As I recollected again my own imagined death, we covered him, scrabbling with our hands; then Marie sang her keening, rough song.

I had those own thoughts of mine, of his funeral, but I listened carefully, when the song was done, as she spoke again, beginning so slowly, building on her voice, "Had I not run away with the trapper, had I remained with the tribe, do you know that if I had remained here unmarried, as I know I surely would have, do you know I would have been one of those women who fucked you in the grove?" Her smile became more serpentine than ever. She said, "As I did lie with you there."

I touched her arm. "How can I possibly share this kind of life?" I wished I had those words back in my mouth, that they were tumbling back down my throat, inside my body. I wanted the words back before she could speak again.

She brushed my hesitant fingers from her skin. She peered at me, under lowered lids, gleefully, with the bent-twig smile, as if surprised at what I'd revealed of myself. My words couldn't be repealed; so I let them go from me then, freely willing what had been unwilled before, suddenly happy to have given one indication of the way I could feel about her. And she said, as I knew she would, "No one will ask you to share. You have nothing to do with me but the child that will be born. And it will be most the child of Orcus Berrigan now. It won't be your child any more. It will be our child, my child with Orcus Berrigan now."

I began to cry then, but she didn't see the tears. They didn't last long. I'd arrived at some determination of my life. At least now I'd ask Pawkittew some questions.

Marie said, "Poor Pawkittew!" Then I believed that

both she and the asspriest would lose something in this new struggle.

We moved toward the camp a league away, toward the journey of the still-young day, moved to bind Berrigan to the wagon, taking down his tipi, the last one standing in the village; and an image came into my mind, of Cantrell. It rose imperceptively until it controlled, as we walked westward, its own direction like a dream.

In my waking dream, Cantrell was more gaunt, older than I'd remembered him from the grove of the duel, the grove of ash and bur oak. He wore a military uniform, part of which I recognized as Spanish, remembered from Cahokia and Kaskaskia. The rest of his dress, unseen before, had eagles on the buttons. In the dream, he spoke. He said he would give me a parable, palpably obscure, as nature is.

He said he'd lain long in the gully, then crawled, unconscious, passing away to wake later and find he'd entered a hole other than that of the vanished gold. He said he'd felt its damp walls with his hands, wondering if the bullion might be there, and he no longer remembered which way would pull him out. So he crawled on, twenty or so feet in all, and he arrived in the presence of the she-wolf who was dug in there.

She lay very still at the end of her hideout, growled low when he approached, threatening him. He lay as still as she did until his presence was accepted. She remained so still, a silver-gray presence at the corridor's end. Only then the sounds began to issue from her constricted throat, over the slack jaw and loose tongue, small whines like gasps, coming harder and harder, related to the increasing pulse of her breath, rising and falling, to and fro to a climax of sound and pulse; and Cantrell understood she gave birth as he watched, and he saw the round opening, the wet ball emerge blackly, like the pupil of an eye enlarging. The first cub was born dead and there were only two more, lives in subsequent falls against the dead child, the small animals squeezed from her womb, the membraned cubs; so Cantrell was moved toward her.

Her head lay toward him, her eyes preoccupied, inward with a child-obsessed stare. He saw, in the stare, that she didn't know him, and he almost relished that. He remembered himself as a child returning home with his dead father's gun—the boy of Scotch-Irish and French descent, his father's family American for almost a century—how he stood then above the bodies of his mother, of his brothers and sisters, for their deaths, from the Indians, had occurred in his absence and in his father's absence of death. He saw the death of his mother in the small Virginia clearing, her brains on their ground.

In the long hole the she-wolf had dug for herself, he had a revenge. He drew forth his knife and struck swiftly as the third cub emerged. The she-wolf snapped once at his hand, bruising his skin before she died; and he plunged the knife then into the soft pulps one by one, even into the dead cub. He carved his crossmark, like a signature, into the faces of mother and children, stroked in two long cuts, each time, the particular design of an ambiguous murder. He rejoiced in his blood.

Moving northwest from the river, we entered the heart of an almost featureless land, figured forth only in the tough perennial grass and in animals, chiefly of the buffalo we never lost sight of all day long. The earth was so flat several cows, at a distance, would resemble a stand of pine trees, or one cow a stand of four trees, the sky bright through their legs. Once when we paused, I lay down on my back, and could see no horizon, not even peripherally, just sky everywhere, so clear that the sun appeared diffused through the air. When I stood again, slightly reeling, the deep-bottomed bowl of the sky was so close at its sides, I felt I could reach out and touch it all around me; while the wind, constant and harsh, greater than ever, carpeted the plains in long strokes, the broad hot currents worked into a weave with milder air between them, coursing above the short grass, this grass stubborn in the shallow matting of its roots.

The dry heat of everything becoming the wind was the medium animals lived in on these plains, and it seemed to me no white man alone could survive there, nor parties of white men—soldiers, hunters, or farmers—on the directionless landscape, not knowing of waters. And there seemed no possibility of water, away from the river, in the land that day, nor was there water, Pawkittew said, in most of that land. Only the Indians, the buffalo, the wild horses, the antelope, and the coyotes could find the water; while jackrabbits, prairie dogs, rattlesnakes lived without it.

Here, I thought, Clark's dream of his people must come to its end, thrown back bitterly on itself for lack of fertile land to sustain it; for there was, I believed, nothing for a white man here, not even with the nearsighted buffalo and all his meat, here only the torments of an inescapable loneliness, in the seemingly infinite monotony, as the nearness of the bowl's edges proved an illusion, where everything of a cherished life became irretrievable in the vast distance. Yet the grass had somehow become tenacious here, adjusted its roots, and I felt suddenly that I couldn't limit what a man like Clark, or like Cantrell, could do if the will became even more stubborn, as the grass had; and, though the land thrown up in dust would rend the soul of Clark's white women and stunt the growth of a farmer's heart, both broken soul and stunted heart had proved themselves tenacious before—now breaking past the eastern mountains—and might on these plains excel in at least hysteria and resentment, extorting something from this foreign land; nerves might excel here, in exasperation.

No, it was too difficult, against both the troubling land and Indians fiercer than they'd known before, to perform what the darker, but still white, men from the south hadn't accomplished in two hundred years. There couldn't be, I thought, any extension into, any occupation of these plains by white men; and any who tried to live here as white men would falsify their relation to the land and fall in defeat.

This was, more or less, what Pawkittew had told me, arguing as if with himself, speaking in the journey northwestward, as our voices were dwarfed in the distance, in the empty places where the Indians communicated with each other, swiftly, by gesture, signs carried farther to the eyes than sounds could carry, this Indian language the most natural art of the place, peculiarly suited, surpassing any such sign talk I'd seen among eastern Indians, their full gestures of hands and arms clearing their bodies against the cloudless sky.

Whenever I rode near the wagon to see how Orcus did, when he and I spoke, we tended, two white men, to speak in whispers. He bumped along, awake, smiling vacantly into the sky above my head. We said almost the same things every time, and things seemed somehow unimportant to say, in a trivialized conversation.

Late in the day, we came on a large herd of antelope, sprinting away before we reached them, signaling fear to each other, and their white rumps remained visible, tails raised, long after the animals themselves had disappeared. We received signals of our own from someone far ahead, upon the horizon. I couldn't even see the exact gestures. Pawkittew could, I suppose, see the signals he didn't interpret to me, given by the unknown Indian's distant horse.

I rode to Orcus, and asked him, as I had so often before, "How do you feel?"

He said, "Better, I think, a little better." Marie was silent on the wagon seat. Orcus looked like a skeleton. He said, "You know, Dutch, Marie says the mountains aren't so far from here. They're almost all rock showing, but there's places there where we could live easy, with a lot of game, deer and some kind of big goats, and even valleys where things would grow."

I said, "Is that where you want to go?"

"How about you?"

"I don't know," I said. "I don't feel any great desire for it right now."

I wasn't really thinking what I said, wasn't considering that what I said might mean something to him. "Well," Orcus said, "at least we don't have to worry about Cantrell or anybody catching up with us out here."

"No, we sure don't." For a while we didn't say anything, but he kept glancing at me as if he'd asked me some question and was waiting on my answer. I said, "What will we do about the gold?" I kind of laughed then.

Orcus uncovered a couple of bars of it. He laughed too. He said, "Wouldn't be any use for it in those mountains, would there?" He winked at me, and we laughed together. I was just happy he was feeling that much better, joking with me.

When I rode back to Pawkittew, I thought I might

speak with him too, but speech seemed, as I crossed the distance, so inappropriate to the day, and I'd found it difficult talking to Orcus. The talk seemed to go stale, arriving nowhere, as if we'd never spoken; so I didn't speak and Pawkittew didn't either, as though he'd talked all he wanted early in the journey.

As we rode on, there was more and more signaling ahead, and, after dark, we came upon a lake, in that apparently uninterrupted waterless land. The Indians had found it unerringly, the small, narrow winding water, lying through a crooked ravine that was only a crevice in the landscape, the lake fed by two small streams where scattered cottonwoods had found a toe-hold, and where the tribe waited, the whole tribe but for the assclan. We arrived to the loud shouts of the waiting Indians, as the antelope clan pointed fingers and lances to show me to them. There were yet louder outcries as Ootway thrust her belly forth proudly, the sound of male laughter increasing then.

Pawkittew said, "Dismount now, and make some sign to them. They know that He-for-whom-we-seek-life has come." I dismounted and made signs of greet-ing. On the western side of the lake I could see the dark outline of something like a cliff, not very high against the night sky. The stars were clear above it. I felt so good that I made the greeting signs I little un-derstood to the stars too, and to the moon rising.

Pawkittew and I sat alone in the dark by the lake, at a small fire. He said, "It's only necessary to tell what be-came of her out of her mother's act, what she did with that. There's much you already know about her."

Impatiently, I actually broke in when he would have gone on with it on his own. "Then tell just what you need to tell, no more. How did she leave her home, how did she come here?"

Despite the interruption, Pawkittew seemed pleased I'd asked him something specific to reply to. He said, "She ran away with that English boy, the one who'd come to them, out of her mother's captivity, to replace the dead son whose brains were on the apple tree. She never loved him, but she persuaded the boy, who'd grown up with her, to take her from home after her mother died, after Hannah Rolfe died, long after the father died. They went among the French, to the fort on the lake, the one white men call Detroit, the one Clark wanted so much, even though he didn't need it after all. That's where the asspriest found her."

He stopped, and I said, "Go on. You said you wanted to tell it."

"I also don't want to tell that, among other things I sometimes wish hadn't happened, I am the asspriest and also, against all our tradition, the son of an asspriest. You see, my mother desired him, and he desired her."

"And what happened?"

"She insisted he kill the English one who'd been intimate with her. My father did kill him, leaving what was left of him on the prairie there. They came together to make me."

"I see now," I said. "So you're both the asspriest and one for whom life was sought?"

"Yes." He dug in the ashes with a charred stick. "Some among the assclan have said that the rite was destroyed by my mother and father. And some have said it was, after them and me, no longer necessary to have the rite. Some have said I should have been slain when I came to the asspriest age, when my mother was slain, when my father departed from our people forever. Yet I *was* the asspriest. They couldn't touch me. There were some who thought the war chief would destroy me if I ever returned. I don't think

Tawnew ever believed them, but they encouraged him to challenge me, directly, and it meant his death."

He stopped speaking, drawing figures, I couldn't see, with his stick. We were both silent a long time before I finally spoke. I said, "I've decided something. I've decided I don't want to be the one for whom you seek life, if there really is such a way of doing things. You see, I don't believe that your people will find the life they want through me. I don't know how to explain it. I can't be of your people. I don't even think you believe all of this yourself."

He didn't seem stunned or even angry with me, as I thought he might be. He said, "It isn't necessary for us to believe as your people try to believe in their God." He paused, then went calmly on, "Tomorrow there'll be a new war chief, chosen by me, another from the antelope clan. In some ways, it will go on, and if you won't be He-for-whom-we-seek-life, there's no way I can protect the mother or the child."

"I'd forgotten that."

"There'll be no harm to you in what we'll do tomorrow. Almost everything has already been done. The assclan has prepared for six nights now; you have already lived the life you have lived in this country; the child has or has not been conceived. If you wish, by this time tomorrow, you can be camped on your route toward the Spanish settlements. I'll draw a map for you to follow."

Then I thought of telling him about Marie and me, but I only said, "I'm sorry if I've helped make these things worse for you."

Pawkittew smiled at that. "You know," he said, "that my people have also called you Fish-out-of-water?"

I said, "Yes, I know, but I'm not that. And I'm not an Indian at all. I'm not even a white man. I don't know what to call myself any more." That was so, but I didn't tell him I was pleased it was so.

He said, "Perhaps the things you'll meet with, briefly, tomorrow, the few things you'll see, will interest you after all. You may be surprised with yourself."

"I have been before. There wouldn't be anything new in that."

Their fire was sheltered by the overturned wagon. Orcus slept, peacefully, it seemed. He was very far from me in his rest. Marie sat near him with a pile of buffalo hides at her feet, cutting into one with the knife that had killed her father. I couldn't think what to say, couldn't say what I most wanted to say.

Orcus moved a little, and Marie watched him carefully until he'd settled once more against the small hillock where he lay propped up. When she looked at me then, I said, "He does seem better."

She said something, but in the tribal language, and returned to her work.

I was shaken. I said, "But I'm worried that he won't be safe." I didn't know whether I meant it. It was something to say, something to move her.

She sat up straight, letting the knife fall from her hand. Whatever she said then, in that foreign tongue, she said it sharply, with anger toward me, and Orcus woke.

Groggily, he said, "Oh . . . what's wrong? Dutch? Is that you, Dutch?"

"Yes, it's me."

Marie spoke to him softly, her fingers smoothing his eyelids. What she said he couldn't have understood, any more than I could. He removed her fingers and strained to understand anything she said.

Then he turned toward me, frowning, sitting up beside her, her fingers held firmly in his large hand.

He said, "It's funny. I can't get her to talk English any more . . . I reckon I'll pick it up afterwhile, don't you think? Yes, I think I will."

"Looks like you'd better," I said. It was supposed to be a joke, an invitation for him to laugh along with me. He didn't laugh. I thought he wished to tell me something else. He'd glance at Marie, who now ignored both of us, absorbed in her work, then glance back at me. He smiled or he frowned.

At last he said, "Well, I'd better get me some sleep. Long day tomorrow."

As he lay back down, I looked at Marie, stitching. I said, "Goodnight, Orcus Berrigan." Marie looked up.

She said more words in her tongue, words that I knew by now, that meant, "Farewell, He-for-whom-we-seek-life?"

And Orcus knew those words. He said, eyes shut, "Yes, goodnight . . ." He never finished, and I turned away toward my own sleep, past the horses, the dogs that nudged me, past the Indian tipis to my own buffalo robes, where Pawkittew already slept nearby.

In the morning, there were dogs and horses, women and warriors, children, the buffalo, always with us, not too far distant now, the sound of the wild horses the Indians thought too instrumental to be their gods (as the buffalo had become almost too instrumental), then the young men of the tribe riding on the plains, in exhibition of their skill with horse and with bow. I'd never seen anything like it, how well they rode and shot.

Pawkittew said, "They'll feast all day today, and all night. They'll almost forget you."

The new war chief, a slender young man, stood beside us, uncomfortable in his office. This was to become his celebration, not mine any more. We watched a youth, his trained horse at full gallop, drive a single arrow cleanly through the neck of a calf. The animal's forelegs crumpled and plowed; the small hump sank down.

Orcus and Marie had gone. They'd risen before us, before the earliest light, pursuing their own course far from us, leaving our gold piled behind them, a reminder to me of our past; a single gold bar lay in my trappings now, placed there, almost reluctantly, for the future. I imagined Marie driving the wagon, Orcus staring back into the eyes of the trapper's trailing pinto, his stallion in the traces. And I said, after the calf fell down, "He asked me to go with them. Perhaps I should have gone." The asspriest knew what I was talking about. He stared to the west, where the red cliff rose.

The exercise of the young Indians and the horses ended when Pawkittew signaled, the convolutions of his arms as if freed from his body. One boy rode up to us on a powerful spotted horse, thick in the withers. Pawkittew said, "This is for you." He touched the horse.

"Thank you," I said. My mare was so tired. She'd had to learn to do without the grain she was used to, eating now of the prairie grasses only. Each of the Indians, even the women, had at least two horses. A fresh horse could be worth their lives. Two horses might mean mine. In the spring before we came, the tribe had fought with the southern plains Indians. I was soon to pass through those southern lands, beyond The-art-of-war.

Pawkittew said the time had come to go from them. When I tried to say goodbye to Ootway, she grinned at me foolishly as though she didn't recognize me. I knew she didn't understand a word I said, as if I'd passed through her and she could no longer hear my voice behind her. Already she'd given me the new clothes she'd made from the buffalo. I'd wrapped the gold bar in them.

Over the rosy cliff, a thin smoke rose that I hadn't seen before. Pawkittew and I departed, circling the lake southward, toward that signal smoke, toward the wind-blown column.

The Indians didn't appear to notice my departure, as if they'd forgotten, now the new war chief was chosen, both me and their asspriest. Their chaste and severe festivities continued without us, as we rode away.

Pawkittew led the way, on his ever-present mule, up the sheer countenance, on the narrow path crisscrossing the rising face, as the encampment fell away beneath us. In our ascent, there came the illusion of a simultaneous safe descent of the village. It fell beneath us, under the hooves. The land at the top sloped down gently westward for a mile, then again became the interminable plains, empty but for a distant line of buffalo.

In the foreground, asses grazed, tethered all about. A large oval lodge, near a small peaked one, stood before us, its hides whitely stretched, tautly over the boughs, over the poles. The asses greeted our appearance, briefly, with a harsh chorus of brays and snorts. Pawkittew's mule answered them.

As though recently, I remember the lodge, a simplicity in the preparation and in the rite, the representatives of four clans who were silent as we dismounted and entered. I saw the four earth-anchorers, the ancient representatives, heads of their clans, playing their designated roles—East at the entrance, North, West at the exit, and South: the clans of bear, buffalo, eagle, and ass. The rite-giver and I circled through them. We sat down between South, of the ass clan, and the reencountered entrance.

The asspriest, Pawkittew, rose among us. He spoke in words I couldn't understand and wasn't meant to. The pipe passed from East through the ancestor-host —the rite-giver, Pawkittew—then to me. I carried the pipe back to East across the entrance.

Pawkittew explained, in my mother's and his mother's language, that each person was speaking to only one person at a time—though each might sometimes seem to talk to all—as the ancestors had allowed. He welcomed the ancestors, through their individual representatives, to the creation lodge. He made the steam issue from the lodge's center, where I stood naked again, and the steam grew upon me between the four bent green poles, surrounded me like a wet invisible skin, like a new kind of clothing.

Most of what was said in the lodge was said in their own language, but they spoke, sometimes, in carefully rehearsed English which was difficult for me to understand, for only the most formal aspects of the language were emphatic in their usage, and their accent was strange. I only understood that they told something that had gone before me in my own life. They said I should learn the truth of my visions and the significance of my own experience. They spoke of five animals and one voice, or other animal, which were to be presented to me as if they were sacraments, things at once so strange and common.

The asspriest brought his mule, the mule I felt I'd known so long now, and, as he instructed me, I beheld it and curried it; I spread an oil on its body, which made the mule glisten, more blue-white, like suns in a dream I'd had. He stood quietly to my touches in the oval lodge.

Then the four island-anchorers and the ancestor-host told, serially, a story of how a strange animal was stolen from the white men of the East as the asses were stolen from those of the South. The animal was almost a god, a revelation from old gods and ancestors, a song or story, a vision beyond the asses they guarded. When they said they would discover this new animal to me, they led him in, on thongs Pawkittew had knotted together, the small stranger, on the mule's gleaming back. An old whitefaced monkey, so strange in this place, so common in himself, looked so wise in his features and in the intricate convolutions of his tail. He reminded me of the French trapper in death, and for a moment I felt glad Orcus couldn't see this monkey-captive of the tribe. The monkey sat the mule as though he were natural there, as though together they constituted a new animal.

The rite-giver said that beyond the monkey was another story or animal. There had already been, present today in the creation lodge, the bear story, the buffalo story, eagle story, ass story, now this story being told that was the monkey. In that lodge everyone seemed to have forgotten the antelope, as if they didn't wish to insist on such an obvious creature. Nor were the snakes mentioned, but each earth-anchorer wore a patterned skin around an ankle, and rattles sounded whenever they moved. One by one, the five men repeated that there was to be another story or god after the monkey, a story in a voice, a god in a story.

One by one, each earth-anchorer rose and said that he no longer desired me to participate in their rites. The mule, released, followed them through the entrance. He bore the monkey, going unguided, as the asspriest, as if in illustration of something I was meant to understand, stood before me stiffly for a moment, then took my knife and studied his serious features, in reflection, on the blade. When he returned the knife, I looked at myself. I felt embarrassed to see myself, as if I'd intruded on somebody else.

The flap closed behind me, over the exit, over the asspriest's face. For a long time I held the reins of my horses, trying to understand how the mule, the monkey, how the asspriest moved me. I heard the voice they'd prophesied. At first it spoke low, almost whispering to me, a voice as of someone very near me, as if someone embraced me from behind, his hands covering my eyes, whispering to ask me if I knew who he was. My recent experiences seemed to foam in my head, and I felt as though someone had been invented just to speak to me, someone who related my own recent past as if it were his own. It was someone who moved now, newly existing inside me, as my past died into me, penetrating, whispered word by word, as if the story occurred from the process of forgetting so that remembrance was transformed, as if a snake shed, not exterior but interior, skins which grew inwardly, newly layered, deltas building from the old skins falling soundlessly in the deep, interior pool.

The louder voice went before me then, receding always ahead as the landscape had always receded on the horizon's curve, receding in the motion of wind and sun, while, in the voice's curled relation, I felt I could almost hear a new name for myself, as though the whole story he told were my christening, the whole relation the name itself, some calling of me never quite uttered, always hinted in the intonations of the speaker. With my two horses, I leaned into the voice I heard, through the sun breaking down in the wind and dust. My own lips traced the pattern, the temporal rhythm of my pulse, a single movement of ascent and descent, beating through its own mutations like my heart, in a world where ventriloquists were natural.

Sight failed at last in the great distances. The voice I heard spread through the flatland like the sun and wind, like the prairie fire, and the land, as if in flame, rose to reveal its figures—the animals, Indians, two white men, the half-breed, whatever Marie was—the voice always changing, casting through disparate objects; and, of course, it was always, I recognized, my own continuing voice, always saying I remembered.

Someone said, "It is when I'm tired and my bones become sharp, in the interior, like long, curved swords and tiny knives, in an intricate relation, exasperating my flesh, that I say to him,

" 'What I most clearly remember, what I prefer now mainly to recall, is the simple naming, precise and elemental, of the visible creatures, as I rose and stood in the margin, in the boundary of the water and the fire, in the thin division where the land surged upward, as in the grass blades, as I felt I'd soon explode to become a pillar of steam, a column of wavering smoke, as something of the marginal had risen in me, as I felt the new pressure of the grass underfoot, my feet still tender on the cutting edges, on the tiny points, my tickled feet, pleasured over the green grass, and my body swayed like a thick trunk in the wind, or I moved through the air like a delicate blade, when my head was full of things, as the treetops, as the animals came, moving leaves and bodies into my heavy gaze, animals opening, revealing their natures to me, my tongue agile in their openings, calling them as they displayed themselves; so I couldn't tell whether they most revealed their own names, or opened most to the sound of my voice, whether they appeared to me first secret and strange, as they would be again, or from the first unfolded tenderly before I saw them, anticipating their names, preparing themselves for my tongue, arranging ahead of time that intricate grain, the pattern I learned to know them by, by which they came into my life.

" 'I no longer mind the closing of the animals, after the first time, shutting like softest long petals or fingers into the center of the flower or the palm, each animal touching himself there with the gentleness of one who probes a wound in himself, the animals glancing up at me as if I'd wounded them; for I see in the closing of things now only another revelation or the new emphasis, now the strangeness of them, impenetrable and dark, that in aftersight was always there, though not fully acknowledged, now the closeness of the animal to himself, the breath's own interior rhythm, the inner grain in them which almost knows itself, the males and females different, one animal different from another animal of his kind and sex, and me now terribly different, and an awe between us, and my gaze more ponderous than ever, and my speech now more hesitant, even if louder, as I watch how the names confirm themselves, and I'm wary of the fierceness in the closure of the flower and the fingers—the flower into a hard, round fruit, and my hand close upon the fruit, gripping it, the teeth nipping through the tough skin, as I did not cease to wonder at animals then.'

"Then he remembers the gray ocean, almost dying, which leaves him high and dry, in America, and he remembers the violence and near ritual of the grove of ash and bur oak. He remembers, after the flooding ground: There was something of ritual in the pattern, something in the clearing among the dark heads, necks of horses like stalks bent over, something rising out of that darkness, under the moon's sliver, above the river, in the grove. Now clearly he remembers, from the high grove's clearing, something falling into the light, his life pulsing among the young men's moving bodies, something of ritual in the clearing, advancing, retreating, a life's fiction, the men looming, remembers above them, transformed, as though he's become someone he must enter like a dream, as if he knows who he is and what the dream reveals, must enter again into some alteration of himself, and, entering, remembers ritual transformations in the grove, the little bush fires burning, the animals coming up, treetops like the heads of men, his slim figure leaning out of one dream as though into another."

A Note on the Design of This Book

*The text of this book was set by Fototronic CRT in a type face known as Garamond.
Its design is based on letterforms originally created
by Claude Garamond, 1510–61. Garamond was a pupil
of Geoffrey Troy and may have patterned his letterforms
on Venetian models. To this day, the type face that bears his name
is one of the most attractive used in book composition,
and the intervening years have caused it
to lose little of its freshness or beauty.*

*Composed, printed, and bound by
The Colonial Press Inc., Clinton, Massachusetts
Typography by Elton Robinson*

*Cover illustration by James Grashow
Photograph on back cover by Morris Dressler
Cover design by R. D. Scudellari*